REA

DO NOT REMOVE
CARDS FROM POCKET

4-84

Illusion

By Mignon Warner

ILLUSION
DEVIL'S KNELL
THE GIRL WHO WAS CLAIRVOYANT
DEATH IN TIME
THE TAROT MURDERS
A MEDIUM FOR MURDER
GRAVE ERROR
OLD GHOSTS NEVER DIE
WHO SAW HER DIE?

Illusion

MIGNON WARNER

PUBLISHED FOR THE CRIME CLUB BY

DOUBLEDAY & COMPANY, INC.

GARDEN CITY, NEW YORK

1984

All of the characters in this book
are fictitious, and any resemblance
to actual persons, living or dead,
is purely coincidental.

Library of Congress Cataloging in Publication Data

Warner, Migon.
Illusion.

I. Title
PR6073.A7275I44   1984   823'.914
ISBN: 0-385-19256-8

Library of Congress Catalog Card Number 83–14241
Printed in the United States of America
First Edition

For Alan

Contents

	Prologue	1
1.	Mad Hatter's Tea Party	13
2.	Queen of Hearts	21
3.	The Knave	28
4.	A Cheshire Cat	37
5.	Curious and Curiouser	42
6.	Another Very Curious Thing	49
7.	A Short but Sad Tale	55
8.	And Now for a Riddle	60
9.	A Question Within a Question	69
10.	Accusations Are Made	73
11.	Lilla Tells Her History	85
12.	The Question Is: What Did the Butler Find?	94
13.	Off with Their Heads!	100
14.	Mock Court of Inquiry	108
15.	The Evidence of the Knave	115
16.	Call the Next Witness!	122
17.	The Evidence of the Musical Director	126
18.	The Evidence of the Losers	130
19.	The Evidence of the Winner	131
20.	The Accused	134
21.	Inch by Inch	138
22.	The Red Herring's Evidence	145
23.	Consider Your Verdict!	147
24.	More Evidence?	150
25.	The Secret Kept from Everyone Else	153
26.	Only an Illusion	158
	Epilogue	167

Illusion

Prologue

The driver of the minibus, a short, thickset young man of about twenty-five with an irritating tendency to smirk when spoken to, muttered incoherently to himself, and the tense-looking, silver-haired man sitting on the single seat immediately behind him leaned quickly forward and said something to him. A moment later, the minibus left the centre lane of the motorway, pulling sharply across the slow lane and jerking to an abrupt halt on the hard shoulder.

Hauling himself out of his seat, the driver (who had introduced himself simply as Murray) then got down from the bus and disappeared round the rear of it. His nine passengers, most of whom had been dozing—or pretending to doze—immediately became alert and, without leaving their seats, craned their necks this way and that in an endeavour to see where he had gone and what he was doing. With the exception of the silver-haired man who had spoken to the driver several moments earlier, the passengers (three women and six men altogether) were all wearing formal evening dress.

Cappy Hirsch, the stunningly attractive, green-eyed redhead sharing a seat with an older though none the less attractive woman at the rear of the bus, grabbed the back of the seat in front of her, then squirmed round and said irritably, "Now what?"

A muffled grunting sound from someone at the front was the only response she got. This was because the passengers were no longer on speaking terms with one another. The relatively mild argument between two of the male passengers, which had begun when the bus had paused to pick up the last of them, O. P. Oliver, had boiled over into a blazing row in the café at the motorway service station where they had stopped half an hour ago, with Cappy Hirsch threatening to walk out on the lot of them and hitch a lift back to London.

By that time, the matter of whether O. P. had in fact picked Bruce Neville's pocket as the latter was assisting him back to his flat after Monday's first night party backstage celebrating the opening of the new West End musical *Abracadabra* was somewhere about third or fourth in order of importance, Cappy Hirsch and Lilla Osborne's slanging match being by far the most vitriolic, despite what was, for them, a fairly inauspicious start. . . .

Smash hit or not, no way, Cappy had threatened Lilla, were her dancers going to continue risking their necks in Lilla's "lousy" costumes in a long run of the show. To which the costume designer, Lilla, had sweetly rejoined, "Oh, I am sorry you and the girls won't be staying the distance with us. Aren't we sorry to hear that, boys?" she had then asked, looking first at O. P., the show's musical director, and then Teddy Cummings, the magic consultant.

O. P., who had been drinking steadily all day, had grunted and made a weak-wristed gesture which could have meant just about anything, and Teddy, who couldn't have cared less either way, had merely scowled and looked away. Teddy had problems enough of his own. . . . Like whether or not Danny Midas, the show's producer and director on whose life the musical was loosely based, was going to drop him from next season's TV series. Teddy had deliberately taken the seat behind Bruce Neville, Danny Midas' personal aide, in the hope of tackling him about it during the journey, but Ray Newman, who Teddy believed was all set to replace him, had equally deliberately (in Teddy's opinion) sat beside Teddy and that had been the end of that. Ray, the show's illusion designer, was—to quote Danny Midas—"bristling with fresh and exciting new ideas" (which Ray personally was capable of building, another plus in his favour), whereas the critics of last year's series had branded the magic offered up by Teddy as stale, unimaginative, and—the final insult—*boring!* (Teddy, who had a sneering contempt for the viewing audience, didn't agree with the critics, of course. It wasn't for them to say what the viewers wanted, or indeed what Danny's show needed if it were to remain at the top of the ratings. That was his job, and he had done all right up to now and would continue to do all right if people would only get off his back and let him get on with his job.)

The current squabble on the bus, however, had finally come to a boiling head when Lilla had sneeringly referred to the show's

dancers as "Hirsch's Hookers." That was when Cappy, her beautiful face dark with rage, had threatened to return alone to London
—and the dinner date she claimed she had broken with a
Hollywood film producer who had a reputation for Busby Berke-
ley style musicals, and who was in town for that weekend only—
and O. P. had nonchalantly rejoined, "So it's true what they say
about the casting couch!"

That did it.

Cappy had gone for O. P. with her arms whizzing about her
head like a windmill in a gale, missed him "by a mile" (to quote
O. P.)—he was surprisingly nimble on his feet for a committed
drunk—and caught Lilla instead painfully on her right upper arm.

The men in the small party had looked on in mute horror,
fearing terrible reprisals, but Lilla had merely blinked in surprise,
rubbed the sore spot hard with the heel of her left hand and then
swept regally out of the café and climbed back aboard their transport without uttering another word. She hadn't spoken since, but
had twice removed her green-and-gold brocade jacket and pointedly examined the ghastly blue bruise that was now plainly evi-
dent on her arm. The wig she was wearing, a hideous shade of red
—on her, that is—was a similar shade of red to Cappy's hair.
Whether by accident or design—she was parodying Cappy—most
of the present company had, at one time or another, been moved
to wonder if it was deliberate, with the question still very much
open to debate.

Lilla, at fifty-four, was over twice Cappy's age. She was also
carrying over twice as many pounds in body weight as the lissom
young American choreographer, though Teddy Cummings, who
had known Lilla since she was a twenty-two-year-old wardrobe
mistress at London's defunct Windmill Theatre, claimed that at
her present fifteen and a half stones, she was now only a shadow of
her former self.

There was something else Teddy could have claimed to know
about Lilla and another member of the show's creative team, but
because it was actually only a rumour he himself had once heard
many years ago, he had thus far kept quiet about it. Nevertheless,
he kept a close watch on Lilla and Ray Newman in the hope of
picking something up—a word, a gesture—that would give them
away. But so far nothing. It was anyone's guess whether the two
had really once been, very briefly, man and wife. All the same,

Teddy continued to live in hopes. If one part of the rumour were true, then hopefully so was the other. Danny Midas could be surprisingly puritanical about some things. . . . Husbands who walked out on wives—and vice versa, for whatever reason—in particular.

The passengers soon lost interest in the mysterious activities of their absent driver and settled back in their seats in an attitude of grim resignation. But at least the unscheduled stop had broken the ice.

Bennie Rosenberg, the writer of the show's book, music, and lyrics, remarked, "Danny's going to be charmed to death if he's been working like a slave over a hot oven all day. We aren't going to make it anywhere in time for dinner tonight. Not at the rate we're going. But then I don't suppose a little thing like that'd worry him, would it?"

Lilla chuckled deep in her throat. "Can you imagine Danny Midas, king of all the male chauvinist pigs, even knowing the way to the kitchen? Want to bet that when we get there, one of us"— she waved a hand vaguely in the direction of Cappy Hirsch and the woman sitting beside her—"doesn't have to set to and make a meal?"

Bruce Neville, the young, though silver-haired man sitting at the front of the coach, turned his head and said waspishly, "You wouldn't dream of saying unkind things like that about Danny if you knew the trouble he's taken to put on a good show for you lot tonight. And you needn't bother yourselves about who's getting the meal," he added haughtily. "Danny's engaged a top French chef to prepare it."

Lilla and O. P. exchanged quick looks, which said, "We'll believe *that* when we see it!"

Lilla looked back at Bennie, thoughtfully contemplated the middle-aged writer for a moment or two. He was a short, fat man with a round, childishly innocent face, and she never looked at him without likening him to Humpty Dumpty, though not necessarily for his physical attributes. Bennie did more moaning and complaining than the rest put together, but was usually careful to avoid any direct comment, like the one he had just made, which the more paranoically insecure of the others—the ones who would use any weapon they could lay their hands on to stab one another in the back, thought Lilla with a small, knowing smile—could deliberately misconstrue as having been to Danny Midas' discredit.

The smile on Lilla's lips faded, and her eyes narrowed. Bennie's lack of venom and sometimes disgustingly sickening overall spinelessness (a degenerative disease, he hadn't always been like that) would have been one of the main reasons why Danny had commissioned him to do the book for the show in the first place. Bennie was one of the best sitters on walls that she had ever come across. She had met a few yes-men in her time, but Bennie was positively outstanding at it.

A tiny, malicious smile showed in the corners of Lilla's eyes. Credit where credit was due, though . . . When it came to the fabrication of fairy-tales, Bennie was the best, absolutely brilliant at setting his lavish fantasies to words and music. And never more so than with *Abracadabra*. The costume designer nodded cynically to herself. No doubt about it, the show was going to put Bennie right back at the top of his profession. With six months' advance bookings and rave notices still coming in, *Abracadabra* was going to do that for all of them. And in all fairness to Bennie, she reminded herself, he wouldn't be the only one who'd sold out for a mess of pottage. This was something every single one of them would have done, for one reason or another. Total commitment or nothing. That was the way Danny worked, she thought wryly. (One of the personal characteristics which, in her opinion, had helped to make Danny Midas the highly successful all-round stage and television entertainer and entrepreneur that he was today; that and his talent for raising the anxiety level in the people around him to the point where he obtained the optimum performance from them.) She smiled to herself. "The Midas Touch," his catch-phrase, was a literal truth. Do a deal with Danny Midas, play the game by his set of rules, and everything you touched too was guaranteed to turn to gold. But once get on the wrong side of him, and then . . .

The costume designer shook her head faintly and frowned.

There was no real rancour in her thoughts about Danny Midas. She had heard most of the rumours about him, had even witnessed at first hand his ruthless exploitation of and utter contempt for others in his profession, and while it was true to say that Danny Midas was a man people either loved or loathed, she herself didn't really have any deep feelings about him one way or the other. Not now . . .

This was Lilla's first time back in England for almost a decade, the last five years of which she had spent working in Las Vegas. She would have been in America now, living and working in Las Vegas, if Danny Midas hadn't been booked to appear there in a show and she hadn't let herself be talked into designing the costumes for the musical he had told her he planned to stage in the West End of London.

Lilla sighed softly to herself. True, the show was a huge success, and it was wonderful to be back home and see all the old faces and places once more—she knew it was doubtful that she would ever make the trip back this way again—but she did wonder sometimes what she had got herself into. . . . A lot more, she was beginning to suspect, gazing thoughtfully at the other passengers, than she had bargained for. She was (as Cappy was wont to say) past it, too long in the tooth for all these shenanigans!

Bruce Neville suddenly rose from his seat, fussily adjusted the strap of his hand-tooled brown leather shoulder-bag and then got out to speak to the driver, who was now down on all fours examining something at the front of the bus.

Faye Gould, the attractive thirty-six-year-old advertising executive sitting next to Cappy, waited until Bruce was out of earshot and then she said, "Don't you all think it's about time you left him alone? I wouldn't want to be around when Danny finds out what's been going on." She was looking now at the musical director, O. P., whose eyes were closed. "Give him back his gun, O. P. You've had your fun."

With his right eye only open, O. P. let his head loll sideways, then turned it slightly so that he could look back along the aisle at her. "I would if I could but I can't. You see, dear lady, I don't have it. Never did have it. The Fairy Queen's been working too long for Danny Midas. It's making him paranoid too."

"What do you mean by that?" asked Teddy Cummings with a worried frown. "Danny's not paranoid."

"You don't think so, eh?" O. P. straightened his head, and his right eye drooped shut. "Glad to hear it, old fruit. I'll sleep sounder in my bed tonight now that I know it's all been in my imagination and Danny hasn't been secretly taping the conversations everyone has with him after all."

There was a peculiar silence, as if no one knew quite what to make of this exchange, but each and every one of them was prepared to give O. P.'s claims about Danny Midas serious consideration.

Thoughtfully, Lilla gazed the length of the bus at the top of the indisputably talented, thirty-four-year-old musical director's head. There was something about O. P. that didn't quite add up in her book. The better she got to know him, the less likely it seemed to her that he drank anywhere near as much as he pretended. For one thing, he was far too perceptive. . . . O. P. seemed to need only one eye to see what was going on around him, whereas Danny could lead any one of the others around by the nose without their even being aware of the ring he had slipped through it. She had noticed how jumpy Danny had been this past week or so (understandable, she and Danny went back a long way together), and O. P. was right about Danny making a tape recording of everyone's conversations with him. At least she thought O. P. might be right. There had been a subtle change in the way Danny talked to people just lately. If afterwards one analysed what he had said, it was not so much a conversation as an interrogation. He put the questions, and you gave the answers. She had picked it up in an argument between Danny and Cappy, which she had inadvertently walked in on one morning during rehearsals, and since then she had listened for it in his conversations, not only with the others but with herself, and it was always there. Or it seemed that way. (She smiled to herself. Maybe the disease was spreading, and she too was suffering from paranoia!)

Nevertheless, it was a fact that tape recording people's conversations went way back with Danny. Almost as far back as she went with him, she recalled. Back to the early days of his career when he was still feeling his way with the brash, often cuttingly cruel line of patter which was later to become synonymous with his name and his magic. Someone—Lilla couldn't remember now whether it was another performer on the same bill or some man from the audience—took exception to slanderous remarks made by Danny about him and his female companion during his act one night; and then, in a telephone conversation Danny had later had with the slandered party's solicitor, Danny had unwisely repeated his comments without realizing, until it was too late, that the conversation was being tape recorded. But for the quick intervention of an influential friend with a shrewd, equally influential lawyer, Danny's career would have been ruined. It was a mistake Danny never made again, and he profited by it. Thereafter, he was in the habit of doing as had been done unto him. Particularly during periods of extreme stress, or if he was getting ready to fire someone and wanted every scrap of incriminating evidence he could get on the poor unfortunate object of his interest from every source available to him—traditionally those who worked closely with the person about to be got rid of. It also meant that he could hire and fire with impunity. (And this, by definition, must mean he had an awful lot of very real enemies out there!)

Lilla's thoughts went back to the musical director. . . .

O. P. had, perhaps, only the one blind spot, and that was Cappy. He was in love with her and she with him. And that, thought Lilla, was really quite sad—tragic—because by the time those two stopped snapping and snarling at one another and realized what was really bugging them, it would probably be too late.

Lilla shrugged aside her thoughts, which were beginning to depress her, and said, "Well, I don't know about anyone else. . . . I keep hearing about this gun of Bruce's, but I've yet to be convinced there ever was one."

"Oh, there's a gun all right," said Faye Gould quietly. "I've seen it."

O. P. stirred in his seat, but his eyes remained closed. "Only in that Walter Mitty photograph he had taken of himself and likes showing round."

"No," said Faye, again very quietly. "I've actually handled it. He showed it to me one day. When Danny was being particularly beastly to him and he was feeling miserable and depressed. It's a twenty-two, I think he said."

O. P.'s right eye snapped open as he looked back again at her. "That figures. It's what some people would call a woman's gun. I hope you remembered to wipe your fingerprints off it when you gave it back to him. You could find yourself faced with some jolly awkward questions when he finally faces up to reality and puts himself out of his misery. Though he'll get shut of Danny first, of course. He's threatened to often enough. . . ."

Faye stared at him perplexedly and after a moment he grinned at her and then "making a gun" of his right forefinger and thumb, he held it to his right temple and said, *"Pow!"*

Cappy looked at him disgustedly. "You can be a cruel pig."

"It's the dreadful company I keep, petal," he assured her sadly.

"Don't call me that stupid name!" she snapped.

His eye drooped shut. "Anything you say, flower."

The same depressing thoughts about O. P. and Cappy filled Lilla's head, and she wished the evening were over, and they were on the return trip to London. She felt suddenly overwhelmingly tired—*old.* Despondently, she gazed out at the empty green pastureland stretching smoothly away from the motorway. Why on earth had Danny buried himself like this out in a middle-of-nowhere village? It wasn't his scene any more than it was hers. Too much peace and quiet and refined gentility would make anyone edgy. . . . *Paranoid,* she corrected herself, narrowing her eyes. It was laughable, the idea of Danny Midas playing the role of village squire. . . . The image cultivated by the glossy magazine features on him and his luxury mansion buried deep in the heart of the Buckinghamshire countryside. Though it was Faye's agency (that is, Faye's *husband's* agency) which usually handled this kind of publicity release. And if somebody like Bennie Rosenberg had written the most recent of these feature articles—the one Lilla had seen—well, the costume designer sighed to herself, Danny's so-called mansion would be as big an illusion as everything else about him.

Lilla sighed so loudly and deeply that Cappy, who had been watching her and heard her sigh, couldn't resist asking, "Past your bedtime, dear?"

Teddy Cummings said irritably, "If you ask me, that driver's being paid by the hour, and he's simply spinning out the time to get as much as he can for the job."

"Danny won't like that," said Cappy.

"And what makes you think Danny Midas is going to pick up the tab for this little soiree?" inquired O. P., stirring himself again and taking a swig of vodka from a black-and-silver hip-flask. "Take my word for it, one way or another he'll sweat every last penny of it out of our hides."

Cappy's immediate reaction, which was to tell him not to be so stupid, became instead a steady frown.

O. P. smiled faintly at her and said, "Never mind, petal. We'll take up a collection for your share if you're feeling the pinch."

Leo Polomka, a soft-spoken fifty-five-year-old Pole—the show's set designer—looked across at O. P. and said, "As you hate Danny so much—and you obviously do hate him, my friend—I am surprised that you bothered to come tonight."

O. P. smiled thinly at him. "Oh, I'm no different from the rest of you. I didn't have any option either. My friend," he added dryly.

"Rubbish," said Teddy quickly.

O. P., who had been left to sleep it off on a couch in the theatre's administrative office during the first night party and had listened with disgust to Teddy begging and pleading with Danny over his professional future, let the retort pass without direct comment. (Neither Teddy nor Danny had realized that he was awake and could hear them talking, and it was an incident that O. P. would sooner forget, anyway.) He addressed himself to the entire party.

"So how many of you have got cast iron contracts with Danny Midas?"

No one replied. Then Faye Gould asked, "What does he mean?"

"Ah," said O. P. "Here we have the exception which proves the rule. You—or rather your agency—has, I take it, that beautiful elusive butterfly—a signed contract with Danny Midas for services to be rendered."

Faye stared hard at him, then looked quickly at Bennie Rosenberg, who returned her gaze for a moment and then looked away without comment.

She frowned. "You're telling me that you, *none of you*, has a contract with Danny?"

"Oh, we've each and every one of us got a contract, haven't we, chums? It's just not in writing," said O. P. breezily.

"You must be mad. All of you," said the advertising executive.

"No," said O. P. "Desperate."

"Speak for yourself, Buster," said Cappy coldly.

"Ah," said O. P., cupping a hand to his ear. "Those soft dulcet tones . . . What sweet music to mine ears. A lady till she opens her mouth."

"Take no notice of O. P.," Cappy said irritably to Faye. "Of course we've all got proper signed contracts. I have, anyway."

"Hmm," said O. P., and Cappy glared furiously at him.

"Y'know, sometimes I wonder about you two," said Lilla.

"Well, don't!" snapped Cappy. "Go back to your knitting."

Lilla smiled nicely at her. "I'm not quite *that* old."

"You don't think so, dear?" sneered Cappy. "Now I know why you squint. You need glasses."

"You shouldn't speak to Lilla like that," Leo Polomka gently chided Cappy. "You should respect your elders."

Cappy shot him a disgusted look, to which he responded with a sigh and a slow shake of his head.

"I wonder what that guy does for kicks?" Cappy muttered, more to herself than to the woman sitting beside her. "Sing hymns?"

Bruce Neville, followed by the driver, finally climbed back on board. There was a strong wind blowing, but not a strand of Bruce's elegantly styled and tinted silver hair was out of place.

Lilla watched him resume his seat. He did so with the ease and grace of a ballet dancer that was fascinating to watch, and she wondered why he stayed with Danny. She smiled to herself. Could it really be true that the Fairy Queen (as O. P. liked to call him) was in love with Inch, Danny's butler, and that this was why he put up with Danny's shabby treatment of him? (Another curious anomaly . . . Bruce baiting was Danny's prerogative; it went on, of course, but no one was officially permitted to belittle Bruce and his ultra feminine ways in Danny's presence.) Or was this just another of those snide rumours that nasty grinning infantine creep Danny called his chauffeur liked to put around about Bruce?

Lilla frowned reflectively. That was another thing. . . . All this talk about Bruce owning a gun. There must be one if Faye had seen it, but that was another of Rapley's simpering little stories about Bruce. She'd certainly never seen a photograph of Bruce with a gun, and she felt just as certain that O. P. hadn't either. He'd made that up on the spur of the moment. . . . Something he did a lot of lately: making up stories, telling tales. Not behind people's backs like some of the others did (if that could be considered a virtue!), and always under the deliberate cloak (Lilla increasingly suspected) of advanced intoxication, which made it difficult for anyone to claim that he was fully aware of, and therefore responsible for, his actions.

She looked from one to another of her fellow passengers. My God, she thought. Maybe it was because she was growing old, and unlike the others, her career was no longer the most important thing in life to her, but what a treacherously dangerous bunch of people they all were. There wasn't one of them she'd trust. . . . *And* the driver was smirking again, she suddenly observed to herself. Another troublemaker, unless she was very much mistaken. Where on earth, she wondered, did Danny find them?

The bus moved slowly out into the stream of traffic. Lilla checked the time. It was six-thirty. She wasn't sure how much farther it was, but she didn't think it could be far now.

She gazed longingly across the crash barrier at the London-bound traffic, which was heavier than usual as this was a Sunday night, and people were returning to the city after the weekend. She sighed a little. It was going to be a very long, rather tiresome night, and she might just as well resign herself to it. . . .

CHAPTER 1

Mad Hatter's Tea Party

The cream-coloured minibus was parked at some distance from the cottage, but no attempt was made by the driver to move it nearer when the small party of dinner guests he had been hired to transport to and from London suddenly emerged around ten-thirty P.M. and streamed steadily back in his direction.

They were curiously subdued, frozen-faced. Most, the driver observed with a smirk, barely said good night to their host, Danny Midas, and his personal aide, Bruce Neville, who walked part of the way along the unweeded, gravelled drive, then paused and left them to continue on alone.

The door of the bus was open, ready and waiting for them, by the time the first of the dinner guests reached it. The driver watched the three women—Cappy Hirsch, followed by Lilla Osborne and Faye Gould—then the five men—Leo Polomka, then Bennie Rosenberg with Teddy Cummings and Ray Newman and O. P. Oliver bringing up the rear—file silently back on board. The driver was tempted to make some flip remark, but thought better of it, contenting himself instead with the look on their faces, which would have left no one in any doubt as to the kind of evening they had spent.

He had abandoned the bus at one point during the evening, intending to stroll into the village for a quick pint and a bite to eat while he waited, but had changed his mind and passed the time in the garden offering advice to O. P. and Bennie who, at Danny Midas' request, were hopelessly striving to dry out the special fireworks display which Danny had planned for his dinner guests' entertainment. Somehow—neither Danny nor his personal aide bothered to give any proper explanation for the sorry condition of the fireworks—the wooden box containing the entire display had been exposed to moisture.

The driver did not go inside the cottage, but from what he could gather, things were not much better in there. The three women were apparently out in the kitchen (as Lilla had predicted) trying to get some sort of meal together—the catering staff Danny Midas had hired for the evening had failed, it seemed, to turn up—and the other men were engaged in repairing a fault in Danny's video recorder (which ultimately broke down again, which meant that he was unable to show them his tape recording of the show they had all worked on together as a team, *Abracadabra*, as promised).

In stony silence, the dinner guests began to settle into their seats ready for the return journey to London. O. P. sat with a hand covering his eyes. Slowly shaking his head, he began to laugh.

"I'm glad you're amused," said Cappy coldly. She was sitting at the back again with Faye. "I'll be damned if I can see anything funny about it."

"I don't think you—any of us—were meant to, petal," said O. P., chuckling. "But, my God, that has to be the best night's entertainment I've had in years. And I bet Danny and wee Brucie are back there killing themselves with laughter. Danny certainly taught us a lesson or two. He knew we only accepted his invitation up here tonight because we hoped for an opportunity to get him on one side and have a good old moan."

There was a long silence. Then Lilla started to laugh. "The look on Cappy's face when we had that power failure and Danny said we'd have to switch over to the old wood stove." Lilla was rocking in her seat with laughter. Tears began to stream down her plump cheeks. "And then when Bruce brought out those packets of frozen fish fingers and crinkle cut chips . . . I tell you," she laughed, wiping her cheeks with the back of her hand, "I thought Cappy was going to crown him with the chip pan."

Lilla got out her handkerchief and dried her eyes. "I wouldn't have missed tonight for anything."

Faye looked at her. She had never admired Lilla so much as tonight, the way she had set to and got that beastly stove working. She herself wouldn't have known where or how to begin. . . .

The bus began to move off, and Faye looked back quickly at the yellow candle-light flickering on the latticed, ground floor windows of their host's home. As a member of the team of advertising

copywriters who were largely responsible for Danny Midas' mete-
oric rise to fame and fortune, she knew better than most that very
nearly everything about the entertainer and his private life was
pure fantasy, but she was nevertheless surprised about the cottage,
even if it did have eight bedrooms as Danny had claimed tonight.
It was more the sort of place she would have expected to find as
part of a larger estate. *Mansion?* It wasn't even a typical English
manor-house!

She frowned to herself. There came a point, of course, where if
one said certain things about oneself often enough, one began to
believe those things. . . . Like all the accounts in the various
women's magazine articles there had been over the years of
Danny and Abracadabra, his Buckinghamshire mansion, and his
devoted household staff who had been with him for years. Nobody
that she knew of had ever been anywhere near the place—to
Abracadabra—in person. She certainly hadn't. Their affair, she
wryly recalled, had been conducted mainly at Danny's London
pied-à-terre. Not once had Danny ever suggested that they should
spend a quiet weekend together in the country at Abracadabra.
Danny had been inclined to be evasive, vague, about it whenever
she had tried to broach the subject, and the one time she had
quizzed Rapley, Danny's chauffeur, about it, he had merely
grinned and refused to be drawn on the matter.

It became all too clear later on, of course, why Danny had never
taken her to Abracadabra, why nobody was ever taken to Abracadabra. . . .

Cappy Hirsch suddenly spoke, putting some of Faye's thoughts
into words. "Well, that was some mansion," she said scornfully.
"The plumbing in the kitchen and that toilet off the landing dated
back to the Romans."

"Did you have trouble with that ghastly wooden seat?" Lilla
asked Faye, leaning forward to look across the aisle at her.

Faye nodded and said, "Don't ask me how, but at one point I was
standing there holding the whole thing in my hand."

Lilla was nodding as if to say that this had been her experience
too with the antiquated wooden toilet seat.

"I didn't know what to do with it," said Faye and laughed self-
consciously. "I got quite panicky about it. I don't know what it is
about me and loos, but I never go into a strange one that I don't
have some traumatic experience while I'm in there. Though to-

night's encounter with that awful seat was a first for me. Usually
it's the door. I've got a thing about them. I can never get them
open. The lock jams, or else the lock works, but the door sticks, and
I get this terrible panicky feeling welling up inside me that everybody's going to go off and leave me there, and that by the time
somebody notices I'm missing, it'll be too late."

"I'd see a psychiatrist about that one, if I were you," said Cappy
sweetly.

"Oh, I know why I'm like it," said Faye. "Once, when I was
little—"

"Spare us the details," Cappy cut in abruptly. "God, nothing
bores me more than having to listen to someone's traumatic child-
hood experiences."

Faye's pale complexion suddenly flushed bright scarlet. Lilla,
glancing at her, felt a little sorry for her. She liked Faye, but
wondered why it was that so often (at least this was in her experience), people like Faye, who were brilliant professionally, failed
so dismally at their intimate personal relationships. Faye could
only handle a relationship with Cappy on a business level. Remove
the business element, and Faye floundered about helplessly.
Cappy knew it too and capitalized on it at every opportunity. Lilla
could see the malicious glint of conquest in Cappy's eyes every
time an incident like the one of a few moments ago arose between
them.

Faye's eyes suddenly met Lilla's, and Lilla looked abruptly away.
Which made Faye feel even worse. She averted her head and
closed her eyes. She had made a fearful fool of herself tonight. She
couldn't think what had come over her, dropping that tray of
cutlery all over the floor like that when she came back into the
kitchen and saw Lilla standing there bent intently over that
wretched stove, face and neck red and perspiring, and with nothing on her head, no wig, only a few wispy strands of patchy grey
hair round her ears and straggling down from the crown of her
head to her shiny forehead.

Faye frowned as she recalled Cappy's reaction to Lilla's baldness. Cappy had returned a moment or two later after fetching
something for Lilla from the pantry, taken one sharp look at Lilla's
practically hairless head and then dismissed the whole thing with
the kind of aplomb (Faye agonized) that she would like to have
displayed in the circumstances. While she had stood there stunned

and embarrassed, not knowing what to say or do, Cappy had merely shrugged and muttered, rather more crossly than was perhaps necessary, in Faye's opinion, "Trust good old Lil to make an exhibition of herself," and carried on with what she was doing as if nothing had happened.

The bus reached the end of the drive and paused. Cappy raised herself a little in her seat and looked back, but their host and his personal aide had disappeared.

After what seemed an unnecessarily long delay—there was no other traffic about—the bus turned slowly out of the drive onto the narrow road.

"I reckon I could run faster than this," observed Lilla loudly.

The driver heard her. Glancing back over his shoulder, he said cheekily, "I wouldn't joke about it, Ma. You might end up having to. . . ."

Bennie frowned at him and asked, "What d'you mean? Danny knows I have to be back before one A.M."

"Does this mean you'll turn into a pumpkin if you don't make it in time?" O. P. inquired.

"A squeaky, pink-nosed white rat, more like," muttered Cappy, and Lilla grinned.

Bennie said anxiously to the driver, "You are going to get us back before one, aren't you? My elderly mother, who lives with me, is ill, and I've had to get someone in specially to be with her. They can't stay with her any later than one, and I promised faithfully I'd be back before then."

"I'm doing my best, mate," grunted the driver.

The bus picked up speed. Bennie listened tensely to the engine, which sounded all right to him, and after travelling two or three miles without further incident, he began to relax. But he nevertheless made a vow. There was something peculiar about tonight. It was too coincidental that so many things had gone wrong. O. P. was right. Danny had put them through all this discomfort and inconvenience to teach them a lesson. And that was fair enough as far as it went. Most of them deserved a good rap over the knuckles. What Bennie objected to was his inclusion in Danny's reprimand. He had done everything Danny had asked of him, often against his better professional judgment. Danny had no cause to lump him in with those other whining backbiters; and if he had, if tonight's little fiasco was Danny's way of bringing them back into line, he'd be sorry. Bennie's expression hardened petulantly. Danny needn't think he didn't know that he'd been sitting incognito through the show nearly every night to make sure that he (Bennie) had made none of the changes he wanted to make to the dialogue. Danny had probably thought he would use tonight as an opportunity to try and tackle him again about the changes. And in the circumstances, Bennie deeply regretted that he hadn't.

Bennie tensed. The bus was slowing down. He looked anxiously at the driver as they pulled up at the side of the road. Without saying a word, the driver got out and went to the front of the bus, peered underneath it. He wasn't gone for long. Returning, he shrugged and said, "Well, that's it, folks. I warned the boss yesterday that I thought I could feel a slight vibration in the steering, and now I'm sure. We've gone as far as we're going. . . ."

Ray Newman said, "I know a bit about cars; I'll take a look. There might be something we can do to fix it."

"I'm not allowed to. Union rules and all that."

Ray rose. "Okay, I'll do it."

"Sorry," said the driver. "I can't let you do that. The procedure now is that I will have to phone in that we've broken down. We'll have to wait for another vehicle to be sent out. This one'll have to be towed in."

"You're joking," said Ray.

" 'Fraid not, mate," said the driver, shaking his head. He noted Ray's ruddy complexion and resolute manner—and that he towered over him—and hoped he wasn't going to be awkward and make things difficult for him. Just in case, he added, "Rules is rules. There's a very strict code governing this mode of transport. There's no way I, or the company I work for, can take the responsibility of continuing this journey in an unroadworthy vehicle."

"Unroadworthy?" said Ray. "You haven't even checked it out properly yet to know for sure what's really wrong."

"There's a fault in the steering, that vibration's getting steadily worse, and that's unroadworthy enough for me, mate," said the driver flatly. "There's no way I'm taking this bus onto any motorway again tonight when I know there's something wrong with the steering. An insurance company'd make mincemeat of my boss if we had an accident. No . . ." He shook his head. "You might as well face it. It looks like we're stuck here, at least for the time being."

"You don't have to sound so pleased about it," said Cappy crossly, moving forward.

Smirking, the driver said, *"Me* pleased about it when I'm the one who's got to walk into the nearest village to phone for help?"

"What about that place we passed a short way back?" suggested Lilla, moving from her seat to join Cappy and the driver. "Surely there'd be a phone there you could use."

The dismayed look on Bennie's face subsided. "What place?" he asked quickly. "I haven't seen a house or a light anywhere since we left Danny's place."

"We passed a huge pair of fancy wrought iron gates a little while ago," said Faye, leaving her seat at the back to be nearer the others. "I don't recall seeing any house, though."

"Neither do I, but there's sure to be one buried back there somewhere in all those trees," said Lilla, indicating her head at the heavily wooded copse bordering the left-hand side of the road. "Well," she said to the driver, raising her eyebrows at him. "Don't just stand there. On your bike! We've got homes to go to tonight even if you haven't!"

The driver took his jacket from the back of his seat and said, "If I'm not back in half an hour, you'll know I've had to go on into the village for help."

"What village?" asked Bennie quickly. "I haven't seen any village."

"There's one about a mile the other side of Danny Midas' place," said the driver.

"It'll take you hours to walk there," Cappy protested.

"At least two," he agreed complacently. "That's if I can't hitch a lift in the meanwhile, and that doesn't seem very likely. Folks round here must all go to bed as soon as it gets dark." He put on his jacket. Then: "I've left the lights on. You should be all right till I get back."

"What did he mean by that—*we should be all right till he gets back?*" asked Cappy as the driver stepped down from the bus and then disappeared in the dark.

O. P., rising and moving towards the door, said, "In case you haven't noticed, we've broken down near a bend in the road. . . . Some unsuspecting person driving too fast and not paying proper attention to his driving could smash straight into us."

"Charming," said Cappy. Then, when O. P. too stepped down: "Hey! Where d'you think you're going?"

O. P. grinned back at her. "There can be only one answer to that question, petal—one a lady should never ask a gent who's fond of his drink. Afterwards," he went on, "I intend to catch up with the driver and go with him."

"All the way into the village?" she asked incredulously.

"Better that than to sit waiting in that death trap," said O. P., indicating his head at the bus. "I don't know about you, but I plan to die of cirrhosis of the liver—preferably in a nice comfortable hospital bed surrounded by swarms of pretty young nurses."

Bennie jumped up. "I'm going with O. P. If there's a phone at that house, I might be able to get in touch with Mother and let her know what's happened."

He disappeared into the night with O. P. and the driver.

Lilla moved to follow him. "I'm with O. P.," she said. "When I snuff it, it ain't gonna be in no pile-up on a deserted country road somewhere out the back of beyond."

Faye said, "Wait. I'm coming too."

Cappy looked at Leo Polomka who, without speaking, left his seat and followed Lilla and Faye.

"Looks like it's going to be a majority decision," remarked Ray, stepping into the aisle.

Teddy Cummings quickly got to his feet and trotted after him.

Cappy stared at them. Then, as if suddenly realizing that she was about to be left all on her own, she clambered down and hurried after the straggling dark shadows sloping away from her.

In the distance there was a scraping scuffling sound and a sharp curse as somebody—it sounded like Bennie's voice—stumbled over the reflective breakdown sign the driver had left by the side of the road as a warning to motorists of the road hazard ahead.

Out of the darkness came O. P.'s voice, dry, cynical: "It's all right, don't worry about it, old son. It was put there for safety."

CHAPTER 2

Queen of Hearts

It took them half an hour to come within viewing distance of the mansion-house to which the massive wrought iron gates down by the road belonged. O. P. solemnly assured everyone that the hideous black monstrosity which loomed ahead of them was Nineteenth Century Gothic Revival of the Early Dracula Period. A remark which nobody took seriously but which none the less definitely heightened the overall ugly awesomeness of the place, the principal feature of which, from their aspect, was its tall, thin black turrets. These projected from walls in higgledy-piggledy clusters, sometimes at quite precarious angles to the ground below and the dark, velvety sky above, as if they were an afterthought of the architect who, having realized that the bleak stone horror he had created needed something to redeem it, had hoped that one more turret would be the answer.

There were no lights showing on the huge mullioned windows which were ranged like two brooding black eyes at either side of the portico. No visible signs of living human life in any shape or form, O. P. was quick to point out.

As the pale moon came out from behind a clump of heavy cloud, a fox howled mournfully in the dense black wood which stood to the far right of the house.

Everyone in the minibus party had paused unconsciously on the long narrow drive, which meandered, without aim or any real purpose, it had seemed at times, through the grounds. They were still some distance from the house and, in the absence of a welcoming light, seemed somehow reluctant about proceeding any further.

Their driver was tempted to mention that he had heard there

was an open prison somewhere in the vicinity, but he decided against it. He didn't think it would go down too well, and someone was bound to ask him why he hadn't bothered to mention it till now. Which could prove tricky . . .

Cappy wondered out loud who lived in the mansion-house. The Lord Mayor?

"Don't show your ignorance," O. P. quickly rejoined. His voice was unusually low and conveyed the impression that, despite his earlier bravado, he was as anxious as the next person not to arouse any feelings of ill will or hostility in the sleeping giant up ahead of them. "He lives in the city, London. Counties are more grand. They go in for dukes and duchesses, barons and earls. . . . If you're lucky, the odd prince and princess."

"Is that true?" Cappy asked Lilla, who said it was.

Cappy gave the house another long, thoughtful look. Then she said, "I don't think there's anybody at home."

"Well, we're not going to find out standing about gawking like this, are we?" said O. P. "Come on, chums. All for one, one for all. Oh, and by the way," he said to Cappy. "If it does turn out that we've stumbled on the country seat of the Duke and Duchess of Wherever-we-are, you will try and not show us Brits up, won't you? The guy in the striped waistcoat'll be the butler. You don't shake hands or curtsey to him. You save that for the joker in the party hat—the one wearing the gold coronet."

"Oh, very funny," she said coldly.

O. P. grinned and started forward again. Alone. But only for as long as it took the fox in the wood to get out another long, mournful howl.

A soft breeze carried a promise of rain on it, and far away, beyond the wood, a tiny flash of lightning briefly lit up a patch of the dark sky. They all noticed it, but nobody made any comment. There were other things on their minds.

Edwina Charles turned her head to one side and listened for a moment to the sad call of the fox in the wood, then finished her coffee and looked at the time.

"It is getting rather late," she quietly reminded her hostess, Freda Cobb. "Don't you think it's time we got down to business? That is," she added in a thoughtful voice, "if you really do need my help."

Freda Cobb, who was probably somewhere around Mrs. Charles's age—in her late forties—and unmarried (she was her brother-in-law's housekeeper/companion, she had told Mrs. Charles soon after the latter's arrival late that afternoon), frowned a faint warning as the butler—looking like something from a haunted closet in a Victorian melodrama, thought Mrs. Charles—suddenly returned to the drawing-room.

The two women waited in silence while he unhurriedly collected up the dainty bone china coffee cups and saucers and placed them on a silver salver. Tall and thin, with a cadaverous pallor, he struck just the right note with the melancholy atmosphere of the depressingly ugly Victorian mansion, which Mrs. Charles had been unexpectedly, and somewhat surprisingly, invited to visit. She had observed the butler with some interest all evening—the manner in which he performed his duties, which was impeccable. In some respects, robotlike, as if he had been programmed to do certain things at certain times and in a certain manner, and nothing could deflect him from his purpose. The one and only humanizing characteristic that Mrs. Charles had been able to detect was that he and Miss Cobb did not like one another. They were much too polite, far too formal with one another for this day and age. There was, thought Mrs. Charles, something unreal about their relationship. As if she were watching not just one actor but two. Neither did she discount the possibility that he had been hired from an agency for the evening. The *nouveaux riches*—and Freda Cobb and her brother-in-law could be fairly described as such—were often far more punctilious about minor details of etiquette (and, in some ways, ill at ease with their great wealth) than those born to money and position.

Mrs. Charles studied her hostess. Freda Cobb wore no make-up and had the scrubbed appearance of a missionary worker. Her brown hair was straight and cut in a short, unflattering style. Rimless glasses and an ill-fitting, plain black ankle-length dress with a ruffle of cream lace round the neck further enhanced the missionary image.

Mrs. Charles had been warned before agreeing to take on the assignment to expect the unexpected, that anything could happen, and she knew she was not going to be disappointed. For a start, her hostess was far more neurotic than she had been encouraged to think and expect. As she understood the situation, it was at Miss Cobb's instigation that she was there. It was she, Freda Cobb, who had insisted that it should be a clairvoyant and not the police who were informed of the death threat which hovered over her brother-in-law's head, Miss Cobb who had suggested that Mrs. Charles should be the one who was requested to look into it.

But after an hour or two that afternoon and an entire evening spent in Miss Cobb's company, the clairvoyante was no more familiar with the matter on which she was supposed to advise than she was late on Friday night when Miss Cobb's brother-in-law had telephoned her for help and invited her to his Buckinghamshire mansion to give her assessment of the situation (and, Mrs. Charles was slowly beginning to suspect, of his sister-in-law). The clairvoyante had been given to understand over the telephone that Miss Cobb would acquaint her with all the pertinent details during dinner the following Sunday, whereas in the event, Miss Cobb had filled the silences—when they were not preoccupied with the food on the plates before them—by determinedly humming a flat, tuneless melody. Only three or four bars of it. Over and over again.

Miss Cobb had not hummed once during coffee. A hopeful sign, the clairvoyante was inclined to think, that her hostess was at last ready and willing to talk.

The butler silently withdrew, reappearing a moment later to close the door. His eyes briefly met the clairvoyante's. His gaze was like that of a snake, she thought. Steady, cold, and unemotional, but alert and watchful. She felt strangely chilled by it, though it told her one thing. He belonged in this house. He would not have bothered to look at her thus had he been merely hired for the occasion. He would have been more concerned with signing off for the night and going home.

Miss Cobb held up an admonitory finger and frowned at the door. The clairvoyante assumed that this was in case the butler was lingering deliberately in the hall. Seconds later, his slow footsteps could be heard crossing the polished boards. Then all went quiet. But the frown remained.

While the clairvoyante had no doubt that Miss Cobb was an exceedingly worried and anxious woman, there was a petulance about her frown that seemed more suited to a small spoilt child which liked to have its own way about things and was quick to resent the slightest hint of opposition from any source. Indeed it reinforced Mrs. Charles's earlier opinion concerning the relationship Miss Cobb had with the butler. They definitely did *not* get along with one another.

After a moment, Miss Cobb said, "I am sorry about that. But one simply does not know whom one can trust. And that man does *hover* so," she added querulously. "I have spoken to my brother-in-law about it, but all he can say is that he's never noticed it."

Miss Cobb paused, frowned. "To be perfectly frank, Mrs. . . . er, Madam . . . Now that I've actually got you here, I don't really know where to begin."

Mrs. Charles took the initiative. "While he didn't go into details, your brother-in-law gave me to understand that he had received some kind of threatening letter and that the following night an attempt was made on his life."

The continuing call of the fox in the wood was hauntingly melancholic, and Miss Cobb inclined her head and listened to it. She seemed momentarily lost in thought. Then, with another frown, she said, "Yes, that's right. Somebody, a man, came here to the house early last Thursday evening—the night after my brother-in-law received the note—and when my brother-in-law answered the door (it was the servants' night off), the man fired several rounds of blank shots at him and then sped away in his car. I found my brother-in-law collapsed in the hall. The doctor said the shock could've killed him. In fact he confided in me afterwards that he was surprised it hadn't. It's not common knowledge—only a few people whom my brother-in-law knows he can trust (or felt he could trust up until he got the note and this awful shooting business) know that he has a weak heart." An odd expression crossed Miss Cobb's face. Then, in a vaguely indignant voice: "They tried to kill him, you know, by frightening him to death."

"They?"

"His wife—my sister—and whoever it is she's hired to kill him."

Miss Cobb accused her sister without hesitation. But she looked uneasy about it. Not afraid and tense, nor even angry, as one might have reasonably expected in the circumstances. More as if she had doubts about the genuineness of the accusation and she either knew, or had her suspicions, thought Mrs. Charles, that someone else was responsible for the attempt on her brother-in-law's life.

The clairvoyante's thoughts were drawn back to her hostess' curious behaviour at dinner.

Miss Cobb desperately wanted to tell her something but couldn't, wouldn't—or was afraid to, Mrs. Charles suddenly realized. And so, instead, she hummed. To do something with her voice other than . . . *What?* Confess? Is that what Miss Cobb was afraid of? That she might forget herself and confess something terrible to her?

Mrs. Charles asked, "Did either of you recognize this man you say came here last Thursday night?"

"No. He was a complete stranger, my brother-in-law said. He'd never seen him before in his life. I never saw him at all, of course." Miss Cobb shook her head so vigorously that Mrs. Charles couldn't help thinking it would drop off. Then Miss Cobb frowned and said, "I just heard the shots and then his car as it sped away down the drive and Bruno—my dog—tearing after him and barking like mad. He will do that, you know—chase after cars. It makes me ever so cross."

Miss Cobb gazed fiercely at Mrs. Charles for a moment. Then, abruptly, she switched her gaze to the fireplace. After a while she began to hum, almost frenziedly. Suddenly she fell silent. "Yes," she said, nodding vigorously at the hearth. "He came because of Jo. That's what it was, wasn't it? He came because of her."

"Does your brother-in-law share these views?" asked the clairvoyante.

Miss Cobb's head jerked round, and she stared at Mrs. Charles as though seeing her for the first time. A chilling realization swept through the clairvoyante. This woman was teetering on the brink of insanity, if not already mad.

Mrs. Charles found herself comparing Miss Cobb with the Queen of Hearts in *Alice's Adventures in Wonderland* and would not have been at all surprised if Miss Cobb had suddenly cried out, *"Off with her head!"* It was certainly the kind of thought which appeared to cross Miss Cobb's mind whenever she looked at the butler.

Miss Cobb leaned towards Mrs. Charles. Her expression and voice were earnest, conspiratorial. "They won't get away with it, you know. Oh no . . . I've been with him for too long. I've seen it all before. Nobody gets the better of him. Oh, they try, but when it comes to dirty tricks, he's got it all over them." She narrowed her eyes and nodded her head, smiled smugly. "He wrote the book."

There was a discreet knock on the door, and the butler entered.

"Excuse me, madam," he said stiffly. "There was a gentleman at the door asking if he might use the telephone. He—"

Miss Cobb interrupted him sharply, accusingly. "I never heard anybody at the door."

"No, madam. We met outside on the terrace while I was out there looking for Bruno. Bruno heard that old dog fox again and has gone off after him. I thought I had better get him in before he started barking. I know how it keeps you awake," the butler added. He glanced over his shoulder, possibly to check on the present whereabouts of the unexpected caller. Then, lowering his voice a shade, he went on, "The gentleman was not alone, madam. There are a number of other persons—three ladies and five gentlemen to be precise, madam—with him. The ladies, in particular, seem in rather a distressed state. They have been obliged to walk some considerable distance from the road where I understand their transport has broken down, and in the dark one of them stumbled on the terrace steps and has hurt herself, gashed her knee rather badly, I'm afraid."

Miss Cobb looked quickly at the clairvoyante. Then, after a small pause, she drew herself up grandly and said, "You may show the ladies and gentlemen in here. . . ." She hesitated, seemed momentarily confused and unsure of herself (or was the pretence finally proving too much for her and beginning to wear on her already badly frayed nerves? Mrs. Charles wondered). Frowning, Miss Cobb added, "Oh, and perhaps if you wouldn't mind fetching something from the first aid cabinet in the kitchen to clean and dress the injured lady's cut knee."

"Very good, madam," he said. "I told the gentleman he could use the telephone in the library."

The butler turned to go, then hesitated. "He asked for Mr. Midas' number, which I gave him, and I understand that Mr. Midas is on his way here now. . . ."

CHAPTER 3

The Knave

Cappy Hirsch, her small, firm breasts clearly visible through the filmy white chiffon blouse she was wearing with emerald green velvet knee-breeches, removed her matching velvet cloak and looked vaguely round for somewhere to put it. O. P.'s brief glance her way took in both the appalled expression on Miss Cobb's face and the disdainful look of the butler as he stepped forward to relieve Cappy of the cloak.

Grinning crookedly at Cappy (who had responded to Miss Cobb's mesmerized gaze with a faintly mocking leer), O. P. said, "What a pity you didn't have time to finish getting properly dressed, petal."

"Why don't you shut up!" she hissed through clenched teeth, momentarily turning her back on Miss Cobb to mask what she said.

O. P. glanced at the third woman in the room, Mrs. Charles, as if seeking a wider audience for his humour, but her attention had since been drawn elsewhere. She was looking at Lilla, who had suddenly appeared in the doorway after having gone with Faye and the butler to the kitchen where a mildly grumpy, late middle-aged woman—to whom the butler had referred simply as "Cook" —had cleaned and dressed Lilla's wound.

Lilla waddled into the drawing-room like a choleric baby hippopotamus. Faye, in a short, beige shot taffeta dress, rustled softly in her wake.

On crossing the threshold, Faye hesitated briefly and stared across the room. She seemed momentarily taken aback. Colour flooded her face, and then, with head lowered and eyes averted, she tried to cover up the moment by quickly catching up with Lilla.

Only two people, Mrs. Charles noted, appeared aware of the fleeting hesitation and discomposure of the young woman as she had been about to enter the room. The clairvoyante herself was one, Freda Cobb the other. Miss Cobb had returned Faye's gaze, then abruptly looked away and inquired solicitously if Lilla were in any real discomfort.

Lilla assured her that she was not, but only too thankfully sank into the comfortable sofa at Miss Cobb's insistence.

Leo Polomka (ever the gentleman, O. P. cynically observed to himself) acted as spokesperson, apologized for the intrusion at such a late hour of the night and politely thanked Miss Cobb for her courtesy and hospitality.

"I understand that our bus driver," he then went on, "has been in touch with Mr. Midas, with whom we dined earlier this evening, and that Mr. Midas has promised that he'll be here as soon as he can."

Faye said, "The driver spoke to Lilla and me in the hall just before we came in here, and he told us he's also been in touch with the coach operator in London. They're sending up another minibus straight away. The driver's gone back to wait with the one that's broken down until it gets here."

Cappy groaned. "How long is all this going to take?"

"An hour or more, the driver said," Faye replied.

Miss Cobb waved aside a fresh burst of apology from Leo Polomka, introducing herself and then turning to Mrs. Charles and saying, "And this is my house guest, Mrs. . . . er, Madam—"

"Edwina Charles," the clairvoyante interrupted her with a smile.

O. P. looked at her thoughtfully and then limply offered her his hand in an affected gesture. "Charmed I'm sure," he said. "O. P. Oliver at your service . . . Monsieur, just plain Mr., or O. P. Whatever you prefer."

Cappy shot him a look of disgust. "Rude pig!" Then, giving Mrs. Charles a quick look and with typical dismissiveness, she said, "I'm Cappy Hirsch, and this is Faye Gould"—she waved a hand in the advertising executive's direction—"and that"—she inclined her head at the sofa where Lilla was sitting—"is Lilla Osborne."

One by one the other men introduced themselves, the last of

whom, Bennie Rosenberg, immediately took the opportunity to launch into a request to use the telephone to contact his sick mother in London and reassure her that he had not come to any harm.

"Early days to be giving anyone that kind of assurance," O. P. said with a grin. "I don't know about anyone else, but don't you all get the feeling that we've gone into some sort of time warp? It wouldn't surprise me one little bit if we're never heard of again."

The look on Miss Cobb's face suggested that she might be having some difficulty making up her mind about O. P. Then, looking at Bennie, she said, "By all means." She looked slowly round the room, frowned. "Though perhaps it would be better if you used the phone in the library. . . ."

The butler said, "If you would come this way, sir."

"It's okay," said Bennie swiftly. "I know the way." He was out of the door like a shot, long before he had finished speaking.

"Well," said Miss Cobb. She was standing with her hands clasped tightly in front of her and gave the impression that she knew neither what to say nor what to do next. She tried a smile and then looked again slowly round the room. "Well," she said, more forcefully this time, "I'm sure Mr. Midas won't be long."

"I think this could be him now," said Cappy who, having heard a car, had gone over to one of the windows and drawn aside the curtain so that she might see out. She half knelt on the window seat and tried to get a better view. "Yes, I think that was his Rolls. You can't really see much of the drive from here." She got down from the seat and quickly rubbed up the nap on the knees of her breeches with her hands. "I've half a mind to make him drive me home."

"You've only got *half* a mind if you think he'll come at that," said O. P. dryly.

Cappy was about to come back at him with some sharp retort when Lilla intervened with a sigh and said, "Don't you two think we've seen enough bad manners for one night?"

"Hear, hear," said O. P. "Humblest apologies, dear lady," he went on with a sweeping bow to Miss Cobb. "It's the drink, I regret to say. It brings out the beast in me every time."

Male voices could suddenly be heard talking in the hall, and O.P. fell silent. Everyone looked expectantly at the door. A moment later, Danny Midas appeared. He cut an impressive figure in formal evening attire, which he never wore without a patterned satin waistcoat. The one he had selected to wear tonight was red with a small black-and-gold leaf pattern. He was tall, sandy-haired, with neatly trimmed, greying Edwardian side-whiskers and grey beginning to show at the temples. He was rather aggressive-looking, even when smiling, as he was now.

"I'm most dreadfully sorry about this, Freda, my dear," he said, going up to Miss Cobb and then taking her hand, pressing its knuckles lightly to his lips.

O. P. watched, amused. The other men appeared embarrassed, nonplussed. Danny Midas was not known for his politeness. Nor for his social finesse. His tough northern abrasiveness had acquired some polish over the years, but not much. He was basically the same man he had always been: uncompromisingly forthright in both manner and speech, totally ruthless where his career was concerned, and inevitably thoroughly disliked by all who got to know him intimately.

"And how about a sorry or two for us?" suggested Cappy frostily.

"It's hardly my fault that the bus broke down," said Danny Midas with a dismissive shrug.

"And the video and the balls-up with dinner and the fireworks," muttered O. P.

Danny Midas looked at him coldly. "You said something?"

"Nothing, not a word, Your Honour," O. P. assured him.

Danny Midas continued to look at him for a moment. Then, looking slowly round at the others: "Bruce contacted the coach operator who's promised to pull out all the stops. An hour and a half—two hours at the most—and you'll be on your way again."

"Oh great," said Cappy. "And in the meantime—?"

"I'm afraid you'll just have to sit tight and wait. And while I appreciate how difficult that will be for you, in particular, you really will have to try and be patient."

Cappy's eyebrows came together in a sulky scowl. "O. P. was right. You're enjoying every minute of this, aren't you? I wouldn't put it past you to have arranged all this deliberately."

Danny Midas gave her a surprised look. "My dear young woman, whatever for?"

Cappy continued to scowl at him for a moment or two longer. Then she shrugged sullenly and looked away.

Lilla suddenly spoke.

"Do you think I might have a word with you, Danny?" she asked. "In private," she added with a meaningful look in Cappy's direction.

He frowned at the bandaged knee.

"You've hurt yourself," he said.

"I'll live," she said shortly.

"Unfortunately," murmured Cappy softly.

Lilla looked at her contemplatively. Then, looking back at Danny Midas and using a curiously imperious tone of voice, she said, "There are one or two things I want settled between us right now."

"Tomorrow at the theatre," he said curtly.

"Tomorrow, Danny, will be too late. By then I'll be on a 'plane back to the States. And what's more, I won't be back."

Danny Midas stared at her.

"I mean it, Danny. Either we get one or two things straightened out here and now, or I quit. I've had it up to here." She chucked herself under her voluminous chin. "That," she said, pointing to her knee, "was the last straw. I am not putting up with any more nonsense from anybody!"

Danny Midas said, "I don't think I need to remind you that under the—"

"So sue me," she cut in. Then, looking him straight in the eye: "If you dare."

Danny Midas stared at her. Then, with a small, forced smile, he turned to Miss Cobb and said, "I'm sorry about this, Freda, my dear, but if you wouldn't mind excusing us for a moment, Miss Osborne and I will go into the library and have our talk in there."

Miss Cobb started forward. She looked alarmed. "You can't!" she yelped. Then, as if suddenly aware of the strange way everyone was regarding her, her mood and expression altered and she added apologetically, "Mr."—she hesitated, looked vague—"Rosenberg, I think he said, is in there." She seemed concerned, unsure of herself again. Then her face lit up, and she brightly suggested, "But you may use the dining-room through there." She pointed to the double doors which connected the dining- and drawing-rooms.

"What's Rosenberg doing in the library?" Danny Midas asked O. P. brusquely.

"Ringing Mummy," O. P. replied. "What else?"

Danny Midas made a deprecating gesture. Then he turned to Lilla and said shortly, "You've only got five minutes, so make it fast."

Lilla struggled unaided to her feet and hobbled after him into the dining-room. As he stepped back to close the door, he said to Leo, who was nearest the door to the hall, "Tell Rosenberg I want to see him off that phone and back in the drawing-room in two minutes."

He closed the door on Leo's mild protest.

Teddy said, "Oh for goodness' sake. I'll do it."

Bennie was closing the library door behind him as Teddy came out of the drawing-room to fetch him.

"Was that Danny's voice I heard a few minutes ago?" asked Bennie. He pushed past Teddy without waiting for his reply. "I want a word with him," he added.

"Don't we all," said Teddy disconsolately. He paused and fished in his pockets for his cigarettes, looking up, startled, when a door at the far end of the hall softly clicked shut.

The man in the purple velvet, braid-trimmed jacket who had come out of what was the study suddenly looked up and saw Teddy. Something close to panic showed on his face. Then, without uttering a sound, he abruptly looked at his wrist-watch, frowned, and then spun round on his heel and disappeared back into the study. Which puzzled Teddy. He could find no sensible explanation for the man's eccentric behaviour. Why hadn't he said something? Why take fright and bolt like that?

Unless . . .

The terrible fears which had plagued Teddy all week bubbled up inside him. He was vaguely aware of Miss Cobb's voice drifting out from the drawing-room, heard her apologetically excuse herself on the grounds that she had not been well—she was recovering from a bronchial virus, she said—and that her doctor insisted that she should retire early to bed of an evening until her health was fully restored. Her impending approach was the spur that made Teddy act. Forgetting his need for a cigarette, he walked swiftly to the end of the hall, paused before the study door, thoughtfully stroked his small black moustache, and then, glancing back in the direction of the drawing-room, he quietly turned the knob and went in.

Bruce Neville, who was seated at a wide mahogany desk, jumped up and stared at him fearfully.

"Don't tell Danny," he pleaded. "He'll kill me if he finds out."

Teddy looked slowly round the room, at the framed photographs which filled very nearly every available space on the walls.

Good God, he thought. The room was a shrine. A shrine to Danny Midas . . .

Miss Cobb paused in the hall, looked all round her. She couldn't see him—who was it they said? The illusion man, wasn't it? The one with the dyed black hair who reminded her of Charlie Chaplin . . . Cummings, Teddy Cummings. Well, he wasn't anywhere out here.

She hesitated as if debating whether or not to report back that he had gone missing, but decided not to bother. He couldn't have gone far. He'd probably slipped into the library to use the phone. And if he was afraid of Danny Midas as the others were, then she had every confidence that he would not be very long.

Shrugging, she walked away and started up the staircase, pausing and looking back when she heard a door quietly open and close.

It was the butler.

"Would you like your warm milk brought up to you now, madam?" he inquired.

She looked down at him stonily. That man went out of his way to irritate her. He knew that, regardless of what time she went to bed, she liked to read for an hour before taking her sleeping pills and drinking her milk.

"I thought," he added, "that as it was getting rather late you might want me to bring it up straight away tonight."

Miss Cobb looked at her watch. It was late, much later than she had realized—a few minutes after midnight.

Abruptly, she said, "No, I don't want it now. Please bring it up in half an hour."

"Very good, madam," he said and remained motionless in the hall watching her until she disappeared.

In the drawing-room, O. P. was saying, "Oh for heaven's sake, Cappy. Come away from there."

Cappy, who was standing with an ear pressed hard against the door of the dining-room, made frantic signs with her hand for him to be quiet. Her face turned bright pink. "That bitch!" she said furiously. "She's not getting away with that!"

Cappy wrenched open the door and disappeared. The door slammed shut behind her, and a moment later her voice and Lilla's could be heard screaming abuse at one another. Danny Midas' voice momentarily rose harshly above theirs, and then all went quiet. The truce lasted all of fifteen seconds, and then Cappy launched into a fresh verbal attack on Lilla.

"I've had enough of this," muttered O. P., and crossed unsteadily to the French doors. He spent a moment or two wrestling hopelessly with a pair of heavy brown velour curtains which threatened to envelope and overwhelm him, then triumphantly he found where the two sides met and swept them apart, unfastened the catch on the glazed doors, and stepped out into the night.

"Someone should go with him and make sure he's all right," said Faye. "He's not really in a fit state to be wandering about alone in a strange place in the dark."

"He's never in a fit state to do anything, but he still seems to manage better than most," said Ray, who was secretly becoming quite concerned about Teddy's continuing absence.

Faye looked round at the other men. "Well?" she demanded.

Bennie said nervously, "I can't go after him. Mother might phone. I gave her this number and told her not to hesitate to contact me. . . ."

"Leo?" she asked, eyebrows raised.

"I think," he said quietly, "that O. P.'s probably better left alone. He'll be all right. Besides, I think Danny would want us all to stay here in the one spot where he knows he'll be able to find us."

Faye went to the French doors. Pausing, she looked back at everyone and said, "You're all becoming as selfishly self-centred as Danny Midas is. I sometimes wonder if you're not a bunch of clones!"

As she finished speaking, she opened the door and stepped outside. She hesitated for a moment, her eyes searching the darkness beyond the small pools of light seeping from the drawing-room behind her and the dining-room on her left.

Seeing a shadowy movement on the drive, she resisted the urge to call out to O. P. to wait for her and tiptoed quickly past the dining-room. Leo was quite right. Danny wouldn't be pleased if they all started wandering about all over the place. Wryly she smiled to herself. Danny hadn't given anybody but Lilla permission to leave the room. Cappy was probably getting her roasting now for having left the others. . . .

The curtains on the dining-room windows had not been drawn, and Faye glanced in as she went by. She could not hear what was being said, but the postures and attitudes of the three people within left her in no doubt that the atmosphere between them was very tense.

Faye moved on.

The wide, stone-flagged terrace to the front of the mansion appeared deserted. She stood motionless for some moments beside one of the two huge stone lions which sat at either side of the steps leading down to the drive.

Coming out here to look for O. P. had really been little more than an excuse. She had to get away from the others for a while. . . . To think.

She still felt a little shaky when she thought about it. . . . Coming face to face with her again.

Miss Cobb, eh?

That wasn't what she was calling herself two years ago.

An emotion more fierce than Faye would have believed possible tied knots in her breast, and she knew what it was to hate, to hate with every ounce of strength in her body. And not just that poor pathetic creature kept trapped inside that terrible house . . .

CHAPTER 4

A Cheshire Cat

Rapley garaged the Rolls-Royce alongside a grey Ford estate car in the converted stables at the rear of the mansion. Then, with one hand slipped casually inside the trousers pocket of his smart grey chauffeur's uniform and whistling softly to himself, he cut briskly through the walled rose garden and then across the kitchen garden to the darkened servants' quarters. He expected to find the butler still on duty. And the cook . . . She never went to bed until she was sure Miss Cobb had settled down for the night.

A mental picture of the late middle-aged, haunted-looking butler suddenly flitted through the chauffeur's mind, and he made a small snorting noise. He didn't suppose the poor old geezer ever retired to his coffin much before daybreak. There was a medical complaint which could make victims of the disease abnormally long in the tooth and chronically deficient in iron, and Rapley—who had heard his mother speak of the illness—wondered if the butler were suffering from it. In fact it was in connection with the butler that Rapley's mother had mentioned the complaint in the first place. "A good blood transfusion might help," was how she had described him to Rapley.

Grinning widely to himself, Rapley opened the rickety wooden kitchen garden gate, then turned to close it. A grunting sound on his left as someone (it was definitely a human sound) stumbled over something, made him start and look round quickly over his shoulder. His eyes, which were already accustomed to the dark, picked out a male form heading towards the swimming-pool down in the hollow, and beyond that—if whoever it was kept straight on, thought Rapley with a sly grin—the guest cottage.

The man's progress was slow and halting as if he were having difficulty making his way in the dark. Or was somewhat the worse for drink.

O. P. Oliver, the chauffeur guessed with another sly grin.

Ignoring the instructions he had been given to report immediately to the butler after garaging the Rolls, he moved stealthily after the man.

No doubt about it. It was O. P. all right.

Rapley followed him as far as the steps fashioned out of the natural contours of the rocky hollow, by which time O. P. was skirting round the white-tiled swimming-pool surround. O. P. paused at one point, stood with hands thrust deep into pockets, gazing into the black pool water; and with a strong feeling of disappointment, Rapley came to the conclusion that O. P. was going no further and was about to retrace his steps.

The chauffeur lost sight of O. P. altogether when a moment later the moon went behind some thick cloud. When it came out again, O. P. had gone, disappeared up the stone steps leading to a lightly wooded coppice and the guest cottage beyond.

Rapley thought so, anyway. But in case he was wrong and O. P. was actually heading back his way, he decided to get out of sight.

He turned quickly and started back. Ahead of him was the mansion, its overall appearance from this, the southern aspect, made fractionally less brooding and menacing by the dull yellow squares of light pinpointing what Rapley knew to be the drawing- and dining-rooms, the study and a bedroom on the upper floor.

The chauffeur paused for a moment to glance behind him. There was no sign of O. P.

Grinning to himself, Rapley walked on, halting abruptly a few moments later when Cappy Hirsch suddenly appeared in the dining-room window. She appeared to be looking straight at him, but Rapley doubted that she could see him. Nevertheless, he took the precaution of remaining perfectly still. She turned her head as if speaking to someone over her shoulder, and he wondered what she was doing in the dining-room and who she was talking to. Danny Midas, he guessed. She was always having a moan to him about something or someone. . . .

Rapley checked again over his shoulder to make sure that O. P. was not bearing down on him. A dog barked hysterically. Cobby's dachshund, Rapley supposed. That dog was getting sillier—and more physically like Cobby—every day. Rapley grinned to himself. Shove a pair of specs on its snout, and you'd be hard pressed to tell the two of them apart!

All of a sudden the French doors giving onto the grounds from the drawing-room opened, and Leo Polomka appeared, looked across the lawn—directly at Rapley but without seeing him—then glanced to his left in the direction of the drive.

"They're not out here," Rapley heard Leo say to some woman whom the chauffeur did not recognize. (One of Cobby's tea drinking cronies, he guessed. Certainly nobody he recognized from the show.) Then Leo went back inside.

They? thought the chauffeur nervously, glancing quickly about him.

Who was the other person, or persons? More to the point, *where* were they?

Cappy, Leo, O. P., Cobby (that was her room up there on the upper floor) were accounted for. . . .

Rapley looked extremely worried.

Midas wasn't out here, was he?

Rapley considered the consequences of his being found other than indoors where his employer would have expected him to be by now and came to the conclusion that he was skating on very thin ice. Midas was looking for a way out, an excuse to fire him. . . . No sense serving it up to him on a plate.

No . . . Safe.

Rapley let out a sigh of relief.

There was Midas now, drawing the curtains. . . . In a foul temper, by the looks of him. He'd been in a peculiar mood ever since the other night at the theatre. And doing strange things. Like this morning . . . Getting them—Bruce and me, thought Rapley—to lug that great heavy thing down from the attic. And then there was that weird conversation Midas had had the other morning with Bruce about dying, what he wanted done with his things. . . . The poor wee Fairy Queen had almost burst into tears.

Rapley looked worried again. Midas didn't really think he was going to snuff it, did he? He'd not looked too clever at the theatre the other night. . . .

Deep in thought, Rapley cast a final anxious eye about him and then hurriedly made his way, as instructed, to the servants' quarters and went inside.

At precisely the same moment, Faye reached the end of the drive. She was out of breath from running and was, for the first time in her life, experiencing how it felt to be out of control emotionally and close to total panic.

She had not encountered O. P. for the simple reason that they were moving at right angles away from one another, and, in any event, O. P. had long since reached his intended destination and started back to rejoin the others.

Faye stood for some moments outside the towering wrought iron gates, trying to catch her breath, which came in quick, short gasps. She felt strangely disorientated, couldn't think clearly. Her heart was racing, thumping hard in her breast. There was something wrong. With her. This place . . .

This wasn't where they had turned off the road after leaving the minibus to seek help.

She put a hand to her head and gazed dazedly up at the gates. They looked much taller, blacker, than she remembered. But they had to be the same ones they had walked through—what, almost an hour ago?

A time warp . . . That was what O. P. had called it, this peculiar experience they had all been going through since . . . yes, ever since they had climbed on board that small cream bus. Danny Midas' Mystical Magical Tour. Only it wasn't that any more—a mystery tour. Not to her. It was all beginning to make sense. . . .

She took a deep, steadying breath and looked about her.

Theoretically—that was, if her memory wasn't playing tricks on her—she should be within a few minutes' walk of the bus. Though she was puzzled that she couldn't see the tail-lights of the abandoned vehicle. She distinctly remembered glancing back as they had passed through the gates and seeing them. The driver, she guessed. He must have switched them off to conserve the battery.

She started to walk along the side of the road. At any moment now the others were going to find out about Miss Cobb—who she really was—and she didn't want to be there when they made their discovery. They'd all accuse her of having had a hand in the deception.

Faye's heart was thumping again. Her whole body was tense and aching. Nothing, she vowed, would make her go back to that dreadful place again. Maurice had begged her when they had decided to get married to make a clean break and drop the Midas account, and she should've listened to him. She could admit now why she hadn't been advised by him, and it had nothing to do with business. It was because she'd always hoped that one day she and Danny—

Faye made herself drop this line of thinking, closed her mind to it, focused her thoughts determinedly on her husband.

Maurice had told her she wasn't to come tonight, and she'd accused him of being jealous—and stupid (to talk, as he had again, of dropping the Midas account before Danny destroyed them, their marriage)—and walked out on him in a temper.

His parting words sent a shiver through her.

"You're not coming back, are you?" he had said as she had gone to the door.

Faye started to run.

The minibus . . . That was the safest place for her now. She'd wait there all night and all alone if necessary. "Oh, Maurice," she whimpered breathlessly. "You were right. I'm so sorry . . ."

CHAPTER 5

Curious and Curiouser

Ray Newman left Leo Polomka and Bennie Rosenberg talking to Mrs. Charles about the show, which she told them she had seen the previous night. Ray was looking for Teddy Cummings, whose prolonged absence was making him increasingly edgy. (Was Teddy waiting in the hall outside the dining-room door to speak to Danny as soon as he was through with Lilla and Cappy?)

As far as Ray was concerned, everything between Danny Midas and himself was cut and dried, finalized. Teddy was out, and he was in. But Ray wouldn't feel easy about it until Danny had actually told Teddy to his face that his services were no longer required. Danny didn't seem to think this was going to be any problem, but Ray felt differently. Teddy was going to hang on like grim death, and he wouldn't give up without a fight. A dirty fight, if necessary.

Lilla, Cappy, and Danny Midas quietly returned to the drawing-room as Mrs. Charles was telling Leo how much she had admired his sets.

Leo murmured, with typical politeness, "How very kind. Thank you. But the real credit must go to Danny Midas. The inspiration for each set was his. I merely carried out his wishes, designed and built them to his specifications."

"Danny Midas," said Bennie resentfully, "is the kind of man who employs the very best and then does everything himself."

Mrs. Charles smiled at him. "Surely not the music. I thought it was unmistakably yours, all of it."

The compliment—which it was—pleased Bennie, and he relaxed fractionally behind a non-committal shrug.

Leo said, "Danny Midas is just one of those rare people who

know instinctively what's right and what's wrong. I personally feel I've gained tremendously through working with him."

"For him," Bennie corrected Leo, some of his ill humour returning. "A person works *for* Danny, never *with* him. Danny Midas has no equal."

Danny Midas, having caught Bennie's final comment, came up behind him and said impatiently, "You're not still going on about those changes you want to make, are you?"

Lilla, crossing to the sofa, remarked in an undertone to Bennie, "Why don't you simply get on with it and make the changes instead of forever whining about it?"

"With Danny sitting through every performance for just that purpose, to make damn sure I don't change a single word without his permission?"

Lilla widened her eyes at Danny Midas. "You don't!"

"He does," said Bennie. Then, sulkily: "Well, almost every performance."

Lilla looked at them thoughtfully but made no further comment. She was a little surprised, though, at Bennie's outspokenness. Danny had finally pushed him as far as he would go. Not that it would make any difference to the final outcome. Danny would win. Danny always won.

Danny Midas glanced round and asked, "Where is everyone?"

Bennie shrugged. "O. P., Faye, and Teddy disappeared about twenty minutes ago."

"What, together?" asked Lilla.

"No," said Leo. "Faye went off in search of O. P., and nobody seems to know where Teddy's got to. Ray went looking for him a few minutes ago."

"Where's Miss Cobb?" asked Danny Midas, looking at Mrs. Charles.

"Gone up to bed," replied the clairvoyante. "I don't think she was feeling very well."

Cappy sat down at the other end of the sofa from Lilla. She looked subdued. (That round, guessed Leo, had gone to Lilla. He'd had a feeling it might, if for no other reason than to keep Cappy in her place. She needed taking down a peg or two; she was having much too much to say for herself lately and was far too rude to Lilla.)

There was a scuffling sound outside the French doors. Everyone looked round expectantly, and Leo, going across to open them, said, "O. P., most probably."

"Thanks, old fruit," said O. P. as Leo let him in.

The musical director grinned round at everyone. "Well, chums," he said. "What would you say if I told you that we— namely, one and all of us collectively together—have been had, had good and proper?" He waved an arm about him. "This, chums, is Abracadabra. And that"—his arm came up again—"that other place was probably—that is, if one compares it with this shack— the dog kennel."

"What are you talking about?" asked Lilla with a frown.

"Perfectly plain and simple to understand, dear lady," he said. "The Gothic mausoleum in which we now find ourselves incarcerated is Abracadabra, our beloved benefactor's country seat." O. P. bowed unsteadily to Danny Midas. Then, continuing: "And the joke of it is that that other place is not two hundred yards from here as the crow flies. All you have to do is to cut across the lawn, watch out for the swimming-pool, climb six steps, and hey presto! there she is, not five minutes' walk hence."

"You're drunk," said Cappy disgustedly.

"Guilty," he said.

The door opened, and Ray came in. "I'll be damned if I can find any of them— Oh, O. P.," he said, spotting him. "There you are. Where were you?"

"Doing a reccy," said O. P. "The penalty for which," he added, eyeing Danny Midas, "is going to be a spot of time spent by yours truly down in the dungeon either hanging up by the thumbs or stretched out on the rack."

"Do any of you know what he's talking about?" asked Ray, wide-eyed.

"I don't honestly know what's come over you lot," said O. P. complainingly. "You should drink more. It clears the head, helps you to see what's been staring you straight in the eye all night."

Lilla, who had been watching the expression on Danny Midas' face, said quietly, "O. P.'s right, isn't he? This is your home. You had us brought here tonight like this deliberately. *Why?*" she asked with a frown.

The butler knocked on the door and entered the room. He looked at Danny Midas, who said, "Yes, Inch. What is it?"

"It's Miss Cobb, sir. I'm afraid—" He hesitated, seemed vaguely disturbed. "I think you should come right away, sir."

"I'll be right back," said Danny Midas.

"The hell you will!" said Lilla, struggling to her feet. "I've had enough of your dirty tricks for one night. Where you go, I go."

"Hear, hear," said O. P. "Me too. It'd be just like Danny to do a disappearing act on us now that we've rumbled him."

"I'm staying here," said Bennie. "Mother might ring," he added diffidently.

The others trooped out into the hall behind Danny Midas and followed him and the butler upstairs. Mrs. Charles looked thought-fully at Bennie and then went with everyone else.

To begin with, only Danny Midas and the butler went all the way into Miss Cobb's bedroom. The rest remained clustered hesi-tantly round the open doorway, each waiting for someone else to make the first move.

It was Lilla who finally said, "I'm going in. I can't stand about out here on this bad leg of mine any longer."

After a slight hesitation, the others followed her.

The bedroom was huge—larger, thought Cappy, than her entire flat—and furnished with what she imagined was probably genuine antique furniture.

Half-way along the right-hand wall was another door, straight ahead of her a huge four-poster bed, lying on which, fully clothed, was Miss Cobb. Danny Midas and the butler stood at the side of the bed looking down at her.

Miss Cobb was dead, undeniably so.

She was lying on her back staring wide-eyed at the tapestry canopy over the bed. Cappy visibly shuddered as she looked at her and then turned quickly away. She groped her way unsteadily to a chair near the door on the other side of the room, stumbling just short of the chair over a discarded shoe. Her face was grey. Lilla did not look much better.

"Call an ambulance," said Danny Midas.

"Bit late for that, I'd say," said O. P. soberly. He looked down at the dead woman, at the peculiar expression on her face. "Maybe it's the police you want. She looks scared to death to me."

Lilla closed her eyes for a moment, almost as if she had suddenly come over a little faint, and then she turned and sat on a chaise longue near the window.

"Miss Cobb had a serious heart condition," said Danny Midas quietly. "If she felt an attack coming on, she probably was very scared. She knew she was living on borrowed time."

Ray said, "If O. P.'s right about this place and it is your home, Abracadabra, then who is she?"

A voice at the door said bitterly, "I'll tell you who she is."

It was Faye, pale, her hair dishevelled, the exaggerated bow on her belted waist adrift.

"Mrs. Danny Midas," she said.

Ray frowned at her, then at Danny Midas. "I thought your wife walked out on you."

"She did," he replied. "I haven't seen her in years."

"Liar," said Faye in a low, menacing voice, coming slowly over to them. Then again, a little shrilly, *"Liar!"*

"This," said Danny Midas imperturbably, inclining his head at the woman on the bed, "is Miss Freda Cobb, my sister-in-law. The older sister of my wife, Jo, present whereabouts unknown."

"Don't listen to him," said Faye wildly. "Can't you see he's at it again? He's lying to you. That's his wife, and if she's dead, he killed her. She told me he would one day."

Danny Midas looked at her for a moment. Then he said impassively, "You—all of you—can believe what you want. Any number of people will verify that this is my sister-in-law, Freda. Inch here . . . Mrs. Charles."

He looked at her, and the clairvoyante nodded and said, "That was certainly how Miss Cobb introduced herself to me."

Faye looked from one person to another, her eyes slowly widening. "You don't believe that, do you?"

There was an awkward silence. Lilla gazed fixedly at her bandaged knee, Cappy became preoccupied with her hands, which were clasped tightly in her lap. Ray and O. P. stared at the floor, Leo looked uncomfortable, embarrassed. Then Danny Midas said to the butler, "Telephone Dr. Kydd, please, Inch. Ask him to come right away."

"Very good, sir," replied the butler.

"I think," said Danny Midas, "we should all go downstairs, don't you?"

Ray and Leo nodded their heads, and Lilla and Cappy got up and went with them out of the room. Danny Midas and O. P., the latter with a final lingering look at the woman on the bed, followed them.

Mrs. Charles moved as if to follow suit, but turned back before reaching the door, crossing the room and bending down and picking up the shoe—a black suede medium-heeled court shoe with a black grosgrain bow—which Cappy had tripped over. It matched the shoe on the foot showing beneath the hem of the dead woman's dress. Miss Cobb's other foot was tucked away out of sight somewhere under the long skirt of the dress.

Thoughtfully, Mrs. Charles looked slowly round the room. At the side of the floor-length dark green velvet curtains and near the bed was a long tapestry bell-pull, and on the bedside table beside Miss Cobb's spectacles case was a silver salver with a glass of milk on it. Mrs. Charles went over and touched the glass. The milk was still warm. Inch had obviously been bringing it up to Miss Cobb when he had discovered her body.

The clairvoyante studied the face of the dead woman. There could be little doubt that immediately preceding and at the moment of death, she had been in a state of panic, terrified. It also seemed likely that she might have been crossing the room when she had suffered the heart attack, that she had tried to reach the bell-pull beside her bed to summon help—losing a shoe in the process—and collapsed and died on the bed.

A small noise behind her back caused Mrs. Charles to start and turn round quickly. Inch was standing in the doorway watching her.

"Will you be joining us now, madam?" he inquired. "The others are wondering if there is something wrong."

"Oh yes," she said. "I'm sorry if I've kept everyone waiting."

Inch looked pointedly at the shoe in her hand, and she turned and placed it on the bedside table.

The butler was at her side in a flash. He picked up the shoe and stooped to put it on the floor.

"They say, madam," he said, "that it is bad luck to put footwear on a table."

"Yes," she agreed, casually picking up something that was dangling down the side of the bedside table and rolling it up into a tight ball in her hand. "But for whom?" she asked, turning to face him as he straightened up.

Inch looked at her, and then, with a faint smile, she inclined her head at the door on the other side of the room and said, "May I ask where that leads?"

"It connects this room with one of the guest-rooms—your room, madam," he replied.

"Yes," she said, nodding. "I thought it might. Is it locked?"

"Yes, madam. You will find the key in the lock on the guest-room side of the door."

"I was wondering if Miss Cobb might've thought I was in my room and tried to summon me to her aid," she confessed.

"I think that would be most unlikely, madam," said the butler. "Miss Cobb would ring for my wife to come up. My wife has had some nursing experience. She always saw to Miss Cobb when she was unwell."

Mrs. Charles nodded thoughtfully and then went to the door.

The others, who were waiting at the top of the staircase, began to drift slowly downstairs when she finally appeared. She ignored their questioning looks.

CHAPTER 6

Another Very Curious Thing

Bennie was waiting for them at the foot of the stairs.

"Any word from Mother?" inquired O. P. dryly.

Bennie ignored him. "What's going on?" he asked.

"That's just what I'd like to know," said Teddy Cummings, who was standing in the open study doorway looking at them.

Bruce Neville suddenly slipped past him into the hall. He was almost in tears.

"I never told him anything," he wailed to Danny Midas. "He barged his way in. I couldn't stop him."

"Forget it," said Danny Midas brusquely. "It's not important now."

"But you said—" Bruce began.

Danny Midas cut in. "Miss Cobb has just had a heart attack and died."

Bruce's eyes rolled upwards. He swayed on his feet. "What? *Dead?* Oh no," he cried, and bursting into tears, he rushed back into the study, closing the door behind him.

"You'd better do something about him," O. P. said to Danny Midas. "And fast. He's having a nervous breakdown, you know."

"A state of affairs which you've done precious little to help," said Cappy sharply.

"Oh, we're not on *that* again," sighed O. P.

"What's all this about?" asked Danny Midas impatiently.

"O. P. stole Bruce's gun," replied Cappy.

"Tell-tale!" said O. P. He crossed to the study door, opened it, whistled loudly. "Would you look at what we have here!"

The others, with the exception of Danny Midas—and the butler, who had gone to telephone the doctor—went over to him.

"Ladies to cover their heads, gentlemen to remove their hats," said O. P. mockingly.

One by one they continued on into the study. Only Faye held back. She could guess what they would find, and she couldn't bear it, couldn't bear any more of this nightmare, *the lies.* She turned, looked at Danny Midas, and then without a word went into the drawing-room. The butler, who had been watching them covertly from the library doorway, drew quickly back as she closed the door. She didn't see him.

In reverent silence, the others wandered slowly round the study, looking at the framed photographs and other memorabilia covering the walls. There were a great many publicity photographs of Danny Midas in various poses, the framed letter he had received from Buckingham Palace notifying him of his award of the OBE, a likewise framed article from a Sunday newspaper colour supplement under the heading of, "Ashes to Ashes, Gold Dust to Gold Dust," featuring a very young-looking Danny Midas in a badly fitted gold lamé suit—the Danny Midas the television audiences of today knew nothing about—an enlarged black and white studio photograph of a strikingly beautiful young woman in her early twenties, several framed awards from various magic societies in recognition of his contribution to the art, and a lot more photographs of Danny Midas with members of the Royal Family taken at a wide variety of charitable fund raising events.

Bruce sat at the desk with his face buried in his hands. Every minute or so his shoulders heaved and trembled, but he made no sound, and nobody took any notice of him.

"Oh, Lord," said Lilla, pausing to read some of the article from the weekend colour supplement. "How dramatic can you get! Have you read this?"

Teddy said, "About the instructions in Danny's will for his ashes to be scattered at sea and the trunk containing all the paraphernalia of his early magic act tipped overboard at the same time? Typical of him, I thought."

O. P. moved up and stood beside Lilla reading the article. Mrs. Charles joined them.

After a moment, O. P. said, "If that corny get-up's any indication of what his act was like in the early days, I'm not surprised he's having the lot dumped at sea. Only place for it, I'd say."

Cappy, who was looking at a photograph on the other side of the room, said, "Look at this. . . . Danny served in the Royal Navy. I didn't know that."

"There's a lot you don't know about our beloved benefactor, petal," said O. P., going over and standing beside her. "Merchant Navy," he corrected her, looking at the three uniformed young seamen in the photograph, the middle one of whom was Danny Midas. He looked no more than fourteen years old.

Lilla joined them.

"Danny was a steward," she said.

Cappy said sneeringly, "How would you know?"

Lilla pointed to one of the other men in the photograph. "That young man there happens to be my brother."

"Johnny?" asked Ray, who was standing nearby. He moved up and took a close look at the photograph. "By golly, so it is. I'd never have recognized him. Whatever happened to him?" he asked Lilla.

"Oh, he's still around. . . . Living in Las Vegas, actually. That's what took me over there in the first place."

Lilla and Ray went on talking about her brother, who was currently employed, she said, by one of the desert city's casinos to spot card cheats and to watch for gamblers who tried to switch dice.

As they talked, Teddy Cummings' hopes sank lower and lower. There was an intimacy between them, in the things they said to one another, which convinced him that they had indeed once been man and wife, the rumour he had heard was true. But he doubted now that this information would be of any use to him in his plan to diminish Ray's standing in Danny Midas' eyes, and he saw that he had been a little crazy to think that it would. Danny knew about Ray and Lilla. Danny knew everything about everybody. . . .

Mrs. Charles came up behind Cappy and looked at the photograph of the three merchant seamen. She picked out Danny Midas easily enough, but she had no idea which of the other two men was Lilla's brother. She thought it might possibly be the one with the toothy grin standing on Danny Midas' right. The feeling that she had seen him somewhere before she put down to a family resemblance which she must have unconsciously observed in Lilla.

"Did you know Danny Midas in those days?" she asked her.

Lilla shook her head. "No. I didn't meet him until some years later when I was working as a waitress in a night-club and waiting for my big chance." She turned to the photograph of the young woman and said thoughtfully, "I think that might be his wife, Jo."

The others moved round her to look at it.

"Nice," said O. P.

"She's beautiful, exquisite," said Leo respectfully.

Cappy frowned. "She doesn't look much to me like her—the one upstairs."

"Oh, I don't know," said O. P. "Maybe she walked into a brick wall after that photo was taken."

Cappy gave him a sour look, but before she could say anything, Danny Midas suddenly appeared in the doorway and said, "If you wouldn't mind, please, ladies and gentlemen, returning to the drawing-room. . . . I've asked Inch to organize some sandwiches and tea."

Leo led the way.

As the last of them, Ray, filed out, Danny Midas looked across the room at his personal aide, who hadn't moved from the desk, and said sharply, "Bruce!"

"I can't," came the broken, muffled reply. "I can't bear it. She's not alone up there, is she? Someone—Mrs. Inch—is with her?" Bruce began to sob loudly.

"Pull yourself together," said Danny Midas irritably.

"I can't," sobbed Bruce. "I'm ill—my stomach hurts. I think I'm going to be sick. Don't make me go in there with"—his whole frame shuddered—*"them."*

Danny Midas looked at him for a moment, then resignedly closed the door and rejoined the others in the drawing-room.

Faye immediately got up and stood at the fireplace with her back to him.

"Is the doctor on his way?" asked Leo.

"No, unfortunately . . . The phone appears to be out of order. I'll get Rapley to drop me over there as soon as you've been picked up." Danny Midas looked at the time. It had just gone one A.M. "It shouldn't be long now before the other coach gets here."

Faye swung round to face him. Her face was deathly white, but her eyes were blazing.

"Liar!" she shouted at him. Then, looking round wildly at the others: "Can't you see that nobody—none of us—is leaving here tonight until Danny Midas has finished what he set out to do?"

"Calm down, old thing," said O. P. pleasantly. "How do you make that out?"

"There's no other coach coming for us. . . . That driver and Bruce never even phoned for one; it's all been one big Danny Midas illusion. And if the phone, as Danny now claims, is out of order, and he can't get through to anybody, then that's the way he wants it, the way he planned it. We didn't just *happen* to break down where we did by accident. We were brought here on purpose. I knew it the moment I saw that the bus had gone."

"What bus?" asked Bennie anxiously.

"The one we came in, the one that broke down . . . Allegedly broke down," Faye corrected herself. "When I couldn't find O. P., I decided to go and sit and wait in the bus, but it had gone, disappeared. I looked and looked, but it isn't there any more."

"I suppose you were looking in the right place," said O. P.

Faye ignored him. She rounded on Danny Midas. "Deny it! Deny that the bus has gone. Deny that you didn't do something to the phone so that we can't use it."

Inch spoke from the door. "The lady is right about the phone, sir. I've just been outside and checked. Somebody has been tampering with it. I really went out to see if Bruno had come back from the wood—there was a scratching noise under the kitchen window, and I naturally thought it was him—and while I was out there trying to find him, I noticed that the telephone wires had been cut."

Leo frowned at Bennie. "You got through to your home all right, didn't you?"

Bennie looked startled. "Yes . . . Yes, of course I did," he said quickly. "The phone was perfectly all right then."

There was a strained silence. Then O. P. said, "Well, isn't this fun, chums? Our catalogue of disasters can now be expanded to include one very dead lady, a missing minibus and driver, and sabotaged telephone wires. This is getting to be a bit like those cliff-hanger serials they used to show at the cinemas for the kiddie-winkies on Saturday mornings. . . . Don't miss our next thrilling instalment!"

"Why don't you shut up!" said Cappy tensely. "It's not funny."

"No," agreed Lilla. "And I think it's high time somebody did some explaining."

"Meaning Danny Midas, I suppose," said Faye. "Well, you go

right ahead, but don't expect me to stand here and listen. I've had enough fiction and fantasy for one night!"

She stormed out of the room.

"Somebody go with her," said Danny Midas. "She's getting herself all worked up."

"It's not a bit like Faye to be so hysterical," observed Lilla meditatively.

"If you ask me, she's behaving more like a second-rate actress than a hard-headed business executive," said Cappy. "Her performance so far has been way over el toppo."

O. P. started for the door.

Danny Midas said, "Take Faye out to Mrs. Inch. . . . You'll find her in the kitchen making sandwiches. She'll give Faye something to calm her down."

"Oh, I wasn't going to Faye," said O. P., pausing at the door. "I'm off to see if she's telling the truth about the bus."

"I'll come with you," said Bennie quickly.

No one spoke for a moment. Then Mrs. Charles said, "I'll have a word with Mrs. Gould."

"If you wouldn't mind," said Danny Midas.

"Who the hell is she?" asked Cappy as the clairvoyante went out.

Danny Midas frowned. "A friend," he said.

CHAPTER 7

A Short but Sad Tale

Mrs. Charles found Faye in the library. She was sitting at a highly polished inlaid rosewood table, gazing at a shallow bowl of yellow roses.

"Are you all right?" asked Mrs. Charles, drawing out a chair and then sitting down opposite her. "Can I get you something?"

Faye shook her head. She looked tired, strained.

"Where are O. P. and Bennie going?" she asked. "I just saw them walking past the door."

"I believe Mr. Oliver is going to see if he can find the minibus. Mr. Rosenberg decided to go with him."

"They don't believe me, do they?" said Faye dully.

"I wouldn't say that. It's a long walk from the house to the road, and you may have become disorientated in the dark."

Faye rested an elbow on the table and covered her eyes with her hand. "I don't know what's come over me. . . . It's not like me to be so—hysterical. And that scares me, because if it's true what I've heard said, and hysteria *is* the mother of deceit and trickery, then who am I trying to deceive?" She took her hand away from her face and frowned at the roses. "Myself? The others in there?" She raised her eyes and stared at the other woman. "What have they been saying about me? They think I'm in league with Danny, don't they?"

"Are you?"

A slow frown made deep creases in Faye's creamy white brow. "I guess I must be. . . . In a way, that is. I mean, I knew about her, didn't I?" She put both her hands to her temples and pressed her fingertips into them, momentarily closed her eyes. "I feel as if I'm going mad. . . . I must've been mad to come in the first place, mustn't I? I'm so confused I can't think straight."

"About Miss Cobb?"

"I can't understand why nobody believes me about her."

"I didn't think you were lying, though I wouldn't say that what you said is necessarily the truth."

Faye looked at her steadily. "Why should you, a complete stranger, believe me when they—the people I thought were my friends—don't?"

"They obviously didn't notice—as I did when you first arrived tonight—that you and Miss Cobb knew one another."

"That was very observant of you," said Faye slowly.

There was a small silence. Then Faye went on, "I couldn't make it out, what she was doing here. It was such a strange coincidence; it didn't make sense. Nothing made a whole lot of sense until I discovered that the bus had disappeared."

"And then?"

"Well, then I knew for sure that Danny had tricked us and that everything that had happened to us tonight was part of a psychological trick to throw us way off balance. He's very good at that sort of thing, you know. And the worst of it is that it never fails to work."

"You obviously know Danny Midas very well."

"We were going to be married. . . . That is, until she—that poor creature upstairs—turned up and told me who she was." Faye became thoughtful. Then, after a pause, she went on: "I knew, of course, that Danny was married—that there hadn't been a divorce—but I understood that his wife had walked out on him years before, and they hadn't set eyes on one another again. And yet—" She paused again, frowned. "I always knew there was something wrong, some reason why Danny never brought me here to Abracadabra. Have you read *Jane Eyre?*" she asked abruptly.

Mrs. Charles nodded.

"That was how it seemed to me—after she, that woman, had been to see me. I was Jane Eyre, Danny was Mr. Rochester, and she was the mad wife Danny kept locked up on the top floor of his country mansion."

"She actually called herself Mrs. Midas?"

"No, not in so many words. She was very frightened of him. I think it took a great deal of courage for her to come and see me. Everybody's frightened of Danny—to a greater or lesser degree. Anyway, she made it crystal clear to me that Danny wouldn't and couldn't marry me because of her. It would've seriously affected his popularity with the viewers—his female TV audience, in particular—if it were to become common knowledge that he'd lied about his wife running out on him, and the truth of it was that he'd deliberately kept her locked away from the public gaze—a prisoner almost, she implied, shut up in his Gothic mansion."

"So you broke off your relationship with him?"

Faye was gazing pensively at the roses again. "I had no alternative. The advertising agency I work for was going through a difficult time, and Danny Midas was—and still is—their biggest client. I wouldn't dream of doing anything that would in any way jeopardize his career—tarnish his image. He—his name—is a multi-million-pound industry. I've lost count of the number of products he's given his endorsement to. . . . Go into just about any retail store in the country and his face and catch-phrase, 'The Midas Touch,' will appear there somewhere on one product or another." She shook her head. "No, if he went under, we went with him. It was as simple as that. Which may seem pretty cold and calculating to you, but there were a lot of very nice people involved. My boss, for example—the man who went out on a limb for me and gave me a job, helped me to achieve my full potential and whom, incidentally, I have since married—would have lost everything—the agency, his home, every penny he had—if the Danny Midas account were lost."

Faye paused. Then, haltingly: "You know, for one dreadful moment there when we were all upstairs, I wavered. I almost believed Danny when he said that woman was his sister-in-law. That would've been too awful to bear. . . ."

Lilla hobbled into the room. Pausing just inside the door, she said, "Tea and sandwiches are now being served in the drawing-room for anybody who wants them." She looked questioningly at Mrs. Charles. "I'm looking for the little girls' room. . . ."

"The last door on the right at the far end of the hall," Mrs. Charles told her.

Lilla nodded. Then, to Faye: "Are you all right now?"

"Yes, I'm fine," said Faye. "Just a little overtired, that's all."

Lilla looked at her for a moment, then nodded again and hobbled out.

Mrs. Charles rose. "Are you coming?"

"In a minute," said Faye. "I'll just freshen myself up a bit first."
She opened her black beaded clutch purse and took out a compact
and a comb. "You go ahead. I won't be long."

Lilla was adjusting her wig in the mirror over the wash-basin when
Faye walked in.

Faye looked quickly away, pretended she hadn't noticed—
something she hadn't been able to do on that other occasion when
they had been getting the dinner ready, she recalled uncomfortably. She suddenly realized that Lilla had been equally, if not
more, embarrassed by the incident, and that Lilla must have been
under the impression that she had known about her baldness.
Which explained why Lilla had let Cappy (of all people!) get away
with calling her Lil, thought Faye with a fresh wave of dismay.
Poor Lilla had been so flustered she hadn't even heard Cappy
shorten her name—something Lilla had warned the entire company, when Danny had first introduced her to everyone, that she
would tolerate from nobody but her nearest and dearest, and even
then only under extreme sufferance.

Lilla was washing her hands when Faye finally decided to risk
looking back at her.

It was Lilla who broke the awkward silence between them:
"This has been some night! Remind me never to accept an invitation from Danny Midas to go anywhere ever again."

"I should've known there was something funny going on when
he invited us all up here," said Faye. "It was completely out of
character."

Lilla glanced at her thoughtfully, but made no comment. She
moved away from the mirror, and Faye took her place.

"That is his wife upstairs," said Faye, running a comb through
her pale blonde hair, then giving her head a quick shake so that
the waves and curls fell more naturally into place.

"I don't think so, Faye," said Lilla softly. "And if you think about
it, I'm sure you'll realize that what you've suggested is quite ludicrous."

Faye stared at her in the mirror. "But she told me—" She hesitated, frowned. "Why lie about it?"

Lilla shrugged. "Jealousy, perhaps. I don't know."

"Oh no," murmured Faye and closed her eyes tightly.

Lilla placed a hand lightly on Faye's arm and said gently, "Try not to let it upset you too much, my dear. You had a lucky escape there. Danny Midas isn't a very nice person. He never was. Take the word of someone who knows."

Faye remained standing before the mirror staring at herself long after Lilla had gone. She felt devastated, empty. She didn't know how she could go on. She didn't want to go on. Life didn't seem worth living any more. It was all right for Lilla to talk like that. What could she know of how she felt, how she'd always felt and would always feel about Danny?

Faye reached for her purse, which she had laid on the vanity table at the side of the wash-basin, opened it. . . .

CHAPTER 8

And Now for a Riddle

"Where's Lilla?" asked Danny Midas, looking round.

"She went to find the powder-room," said Cappy, helping herself liberally to the sandwiches on the tray that Inch held out to her and piling them up on her plate.

"She's been gone rather a long time, hasn't she?" Danny remarked.

Cappy shrugged and bit into a sandwich, screwed up her nose. The sandwich had a tomato filling, which she loathed. Carefully, she removed the offending ingredient and handed it back to Inch, who took it without batting an eyelid. Then she said, "Maybe she's casing the joint. You've got the family silver locked up, I hope."

Danny Midas gave her an irritable look. "Go and find her, Cappy. Tell her the tea's getting cold."

Cappy shot him a look, but put down her plate and did as she was told. She backed out of the room bowing. "Oh yes, O Lord and Master. Your word is my command, O Most Wonderful One. Shall I trot out to the road and fetch O. P. and Bennie while I'm about it? And what about Brucie? Shall I wipe his nose and dry his tears for him too?"

Scowling, she opened the door and disappeared. A moment later, the door reopened, and her head appeared around it.

"Where is it?" she asked. "The john?"

Danny Midas told her, and she disappeared again. She wasn't gone for very long. The door suddenly opened again, her head reappeared and then the forefinger she used to beckon to Inch.

"What's wrong now?" asked Danny Midas, glancing round and seeing her.

"The silly bitch has gone and got herself stuck in the loo. I can't get the door open from the outside. I need some help."

Danny Midas nodded to Inch, who put down the sandwich tray and followed her to the cloakroom.

"Aid is at hand," Cappy sang out loudly as they went in. "The cavalry's arrived."

Inch crossed to the toilet door and tried the knob. The door moved a fraction and then refused to budge any further.

Cappy went up to the mirror over the wash-basin and watched his reflected efforts to force the door. "God," she murmured to herself. "Some people lead exciting lives!"

She turned to him and asked, "Shall I send for a battering ram?"

He grunted softly, straightened his narrow back. "I rather think there's not so much wrong with the door as with Miss Osborne. The door isn't stuck, someone's lying against it." He angled his right shoulder into the door, pushed with all of his might.

Cappy frowned at him. "That's not Miss Osborne. You'd have no hope if it was that great tub of lard stuck in there. It's Faye—Mrs. Gould. I couldn't find Lilla."

"I think she's fainted," he said. "Perhaps, if you wouldn't mind giving me a hand, miss . . ."

Cappy shrugged. "She must've panicked, passed out when she couldn't get the door open." Then, eyeing the door, which was solid oak, she changed her mind about assisting him and turned quickly away. "I'd better get some help. . . . One of the men."

She returned with Danny Midas and Leo Polomka. Leo, who was an inch or two taller than the other two men and more heavily built, said, "Here, stand aside. I'll do it."

He got the door open with one good shove. The opening of the door swept Faye back against the wall. She lay on her side with her face turned towards the floor. Leo got down quickly and raised her head so that he could see her face. There was a neat round hole centred between her eyes. Blood congealed in a fine, lacy frill round its edges and travelled in a thin, wavering line down her straight nose. Her eyes were open and fixed in a lifeless stare.

Leo murmured something softly in Polish.

"What is it?" asked Danny Midas, coming up behind him.

Leo did not reply. He stepped aside, and Danny Midas looked down at Faye. The colour drained from his face. Wedged between her right hand and her right knee was a small gun.

"My God," whispered Leo, following Danny Midas' transfixed gaze. "She's killed herself."

Danny Midas turned abruptly aside, hung his head a little, and frowned.

"What is it?" asked Cappy, a sharp edge of fear to her voice. "What's happened to Faye?"

She moved forward to see for herself, but Inch barred her way.

"I don't really think you should look, miss," he said.

She ducked round him.

"Faye?" she called. Then, seeing her on the toilet floor, the little round hole above the bridge of her nose: *"Oh no . . ."*

Leo took her by the arm and turned her around. "Go back to the others, Cappy. This is no place for you now."

She looked back desperately over her shoulder as he gently propelled her towards the door. Then, suddenly, her whole body went rigid. "Lilla," she said. Her voice rose sharply. "Where's Lilla?"

"Didn't you find her?" asked Leo, releasing her.

She turned and looked at Danny Midas, who had raised his head questioningly.

"No," she said. "Faye was the only one in here."

"Maybe she went looking for O. P. and Bennie," suggested Leo.

"With that leg of hers?" snapped Cappy. She covered her mouth with her hands. She was close to tears.

"We'll find her," Leo gently assured her, slipping a comforting arm around her shoulders. "She'll be all right. Lilla can take care of herself. Now come along, there's a good girl."

The door suddenly opened, and Mrs. Charles and Ray Newman came in, followed a moment later by Teddy Cummings.

"What's going on?" asked Ray, looking at Leo. "Is Lilla okay?"

Leo frowned a warning at him.

"We can't find her," said Cappy, her tone short and terse. "She's disappeared."

"Where's Mrs. Gould?" asked Mrs. Charles, glancing at the beaded clutch purse on the vanity table. "That's her purse, isn't it?"

No one answered. Ray, seeing the fraught look on Cappy's face, turned to Danny Midas and asked, "Where's Faye?"

Danny Midas indicated his head over his shoulder. "In there."

Ray moved forward. Mrs. Charles—and, after a second's hesitation, Teddy—followed him.

Ray stepped inside the toilet, looked round the door at Faye, and stepped back out again. Then, without a word, he crossed to the wash-basin and with his hands gripping its rim, leaned heavily on it.

Mrs. Charles looked hesitantly at Danny Midas.

"Faye's shot herself," he said. "I wouldn't look if I were you."

Teddy blanched and backed away. Mrs. Charles paused for a moment and then went in. Turning slightly and using the toe of her shoe, she carefully nudged the door out of the way so that she had a clear view of Faye. As the door began to close, she heard someone—Teddy Cummings, she thought—ask, "What's she doing? Faye is dead, isn't she?" The clairvoyante did not hear anyone reply.

She got down, looked closely at the dead woman's face, into her eyes, then at the gun, which was under rather than in her right hand and had probably slipped from her grasp after she had fired it and then fallen to the floor with her.

Faye's grey-green eyes gazed back at her helplessly—but without any fear—and a terrible sadness came over the clairvoyante that she had failed to realize that Faye had been more depressed and desperate about the heartless, though perhaps understandable, trick which Freda Cobb had played on her than merely temporarily hysterical over the unpleasant ordeal which Danny Midas had put her and the others through tonight. That because of her lack of insight, a beautiful young woman with everything to live for was now dead. In the frame of mind it would now seem obvious that Faye had been in, she should not have been left on her own for one single instant.

Sighing a little, Mrs. Charles placed her right hand on the cold ceramic tiled floor, then twisting slightly towards the partly open door, she straightened her arm and used it to lever herself up onto her feet. As she rose, a small round hole beneath the brass lock on the door caught her eye. Puzzled, she leaned forward and examined it closely, compared it with the bullet wound in Faye's head. Frowning thoughtfully, she straightened up, stepped back a little, and again used the toe of her shoe to move the door aside. With the door as wide open as Faye's body would permit, she then bent over and looked at the wood beneath the knob on the outside of the door.

"What are you looking at?" asked Danny Midas, coming up to her.

"The door," she replied distantly.

"I can see that," he said. "What's wrong with it?"

"On this side, nothing that I can see," she replied, straightening up to face him. "I'm no ballistics expert—in fact, I know nothing at all about guns—but I rather think someone has fired a bullet into the other side of the door. . . . An inch or two underneath the lock," she added as Danny Midas moved round her to see for himself.

Ray raised his head and looked round slowly. Cappy, Teddy, and Leo moved up closer, awaiting Danny Midas' opinion. Only Inch, the clairvoyante noted, showed little or no interest in her discovery. Though it was not impossible that this was the butler's natural inclination and the clairvoyante, after her earlier observations of him, was therefore careful not to read too much into his apparent indifference.

"Well?" asked Teddy. "Is she right?"

Danny Midas took a moment or two to respond. "Yes. There's what appears to be a bullet hole here."

"Let me see," said Ray. He squeezed into the toilet with him. The door closed. The others watched it, waited.

Several minutes passed before Ray and Danny Midas re-emerged. Ray came out first. "It's a bullet hole all right," he said. "Faye fired the gun twice, once into the door and the second time —" He didn't finish. Then, shrugging: "Maybe she wasn't sure how the gun handled, and she didn't want any mistakes. . . . I mean," he added awkwardly, frowning, "it would've been dreadful if she'd only maimed herself . . . finished up a useless vegetable or blind. That's the risk with that sort of firearm, you know. She might've only blinded herself." His voice tailed off lamely.

Cappy said quietly, "No, it wasn't like that. It happened again. She got stuck in there and panicked when she couldn't get the door open. She was telling Lilla and me about it earlier on the bus —how it was always happening to her in strange loos."

"You mean she fired the gun at the door—or rather the lock, I suppose—" said Teddy, frowning, "missed the lock in her panic, and then lost her head completely and turned the gun on herself?'" He seemed very doubtful about it.

Ray said, "It seems a crazy thing to do, but then I don't think any of us could say she'd been behaving very rationally. . . . The scene she made up in the bedroom, and then that outburst in the drawing-room a short while ago about the bus. . . ." His voice faded away into a subdued silence.

After a moment, Danny Midas said, "But she couldn't have got locked in there. There's no key to that door, is there, Inch?"

The butler shook his head. "Not to my knowledge, sir. I've never seen one, though I daresay there could be one lying about somewhere."

Cappy frowned. "I don't think it would've made much difference—locked or unlocked. Apparently Faye often had trouble with toilet doors. She made it sound as though it was some sort of psychological hang-up with her. She was afraid of toilet doors the way some people are of heights and spiders or open spaces." Cappy paused. Then: "Maybe she thought the door opened outwards instead of inwards, and her brain froze and she couldn't think to try pulling the door towards her. I've had that happen to me, and for the minute I haven't been able to figure out what was wrong, why I couldn't get the door open."

There was a thoughtful silence. Then Mrs. Charles said, "But surely Mrs. Gould wasn't in the habit of carrying a gun about with her to shoot her way out of toilets if she got stuck in one."

Everyone stared at her.

She widened her eyes. "Well, it seems to me that there must have been some other more sensible reason for her to own a gun and carry it about with her."

Cappy frowned again, then glanced nervously at Danny Midas and said, "Well, actually, it's not Faye's gun. At least I don't think it's hers. It belongs to Bruce."

"My personal aide," Danny explained to Mrs. Charles. "It certainly looks very similar to the one he owns."

"Yes," said Ray, nodding. "That's just what I was thinking."

"I wonder what Faye was doing with it," said Danny Midas slowly.

Cappy and Ray looked at each other uncomfortably. "I guess Faye stole it," Ray said to her. "It wasn't O. P. after all."

Ray looked at Danny Midas and explained. "Somebody stole the gun from Bruce either during or after the party on Monday night, and we—and that includes Bruce himself—naturally thought it was O. P. You know what he's like," Ray finished with a shrug.

"Why wasn't I told about this?" asked Danny Midas crossly.

"I'm surprised you didn't know about it," said Cappy offhandedly. "Bruce is usually the first to go running back to you telling tales. Or the grey worm," she added in a sneering reference to Rapley, the chauffeur. "I started to tell you a little while ago. . . . When we all came back downstairs."

"I think, in the circumstances, we should all put our personal grievances and differences aside and keep everything as much as possible on an adult level, don't you?" said Leo quietly. He looked at Danny Midas. "You'll have to call the police."

Danny Midas nodded.

"The phone, sir," Inch reminded him. "We have no way of contacting them other than by your sending someone, Rapley, to fetch them."

"What about that place O. P. was talking about when he came back a short time ago?" asked Ray.

"The guest cottage?" Danny Midas shook his head. "The phone there is only an extension line. All outgoing and incoming calls go through here."

At the mention of the guest cottage, Cappy's face had darkened. "You know what you are, don't you? This is all your fault!"

Teddy said quickly, "Leave it alone, Cappy. I think we've all had enough for one night."

She glared at him, then turned and stalked to the door.

"Where d'you think you're going?" Danny Midas called after her.

"To find Lilla," she said abruptly. "Or have you forgotten. She's still missing. . . ."

He frowned. "Yes, yes, of course . . . First we must find Lilla. In fact, I think we should get everyone together—tell the others what has happened—and then I'll send Rapley for the police." He hesitated. "He'll have to go into town—Markethampton will be nearest. The village is no good; there's only a lock-up post office—nobody'll be there until nine in the morning—and the publican of the Red Cockerel is as deaf as a post. It'd be a waste of time banging on his door and trying to raise him."

They moved out into the hall. Cappy had gone on ahead. She

was standing in the middle of it. She looked all round her, then up the massive staircase, cupped her hands round her mouth, and bawled out, *"Lilla!"*

"Really, Cappy," said Danny Midas reprovingly. "I hardly think that was necessary."

"What did you have in mind? Search parties equipped with maps and compasses? Or maybe you expected us to wait until the official guide turns up in the morning and then let him take us round with the rest of the ticket-buying public. I mean, you do have an official guide, don't you? All the best places do."

"You're being very tiresome tonight," he sighed.

The study door opened, and Lilla appeared. "What on earth is going on?" she asked crossly. "Who was that I heard shouting my name?"

Cappy gave her a venomous look. "I might've known you'd still be alive and kicking!" Then she spun around on her heel and marched off back to the drawing-room, slamming the door behind her.

"We were looking for you," said Teddy.

"So?" she said. Her eyebrows rose. "Now you've found me."

"Faye's dead, Lilla," said Leo soberly.

She looked at him. "Rubbish," she said briskly. "I was only talking to her a few minutes ago. In there," she said, pointing at the cloakroom.

Ray said, "She's shot herself with Bruce's gun."

She stared at him, then quickly closed the study door behind her so that the man within could not hear what was being said. She frowned. "When?"

Danny Midas said, "We don't know. It must've happened soon after you came out and left her on her own. Did she go into the toilet while you were still in there with her?"

"No. The last I saw of her she was standing in front of the mirror combing her hair." Lilla's frown deepened. "I never heard any-thing—a shot, I mean."

"You wouldn't . . . Not from that kind of small hand-gun," said Danny Midas. "The doors are too thick for the sound to travel far. You might possibly have heard something if it had happened while you were out here in the hall, crossing to the study, but I think it unlikely. You would've had to be listening for it to hear it."

Ray asked Lilla, "How did she seem to you? Did she say anything?"

Lilla shrugged. "She was pretty upset. I—" She broke off and looked round suddenly as the study door opened.

"What's happened?" asked Bruce. His face was pale and tense. "Somebody said something about my gun. Who found it?"

"Faye," said Lilla.

"O. P. gave it to her?" asked Bruce, puzzled.

Lilla looked uncomfortable. "I don't know how she got hold of it, Bruce." She glanced at Danny Midas, who looked away as if he found the whole matter suddenly thoroughly distasteful. Then she said hesitantly, "There's been an accident."

"With my gun?" Bruce looked round at everybody incomprehensibly. "Somebody's been hurt?"

"Faye's dead," said Lilla. Then, hastily: "Now don't upset yourself. It wasn't your fault."

"Of course it was his fault," said Danny Midas with an impatient gesture. "I told him months ago to get rid of that gun." He looked at Bruce. "Why you needed the damned thing I'll never know. You've no money, your miserable life certainly isn't worth much, and if it's your virginity you're worried about, you'd do better protecting that with one of the shotguns in the gun cupboard. Though I daresay that'd be a bit too macho for a delicate creature like you."

Bruce's hands flew to his face, and he turned and rushed back into the study.

"That wasn't necessary, Danny," said Leo. "He's walking on a knife-edge."

"He's not the only one," said Danny Midas. He turned to Inch. "Tell Rapley to get out the estate car and go into town and fetch the police. Oh, and if the others haven't returned yet, tell him to watch out for them and send them back." He scowled at Leo and then at Ray and the rest of them. "I don't want any of you wandering about the place any more tonight. There have been enough"— he paused slightly—"accidents for one night."

CHAPTER 9

A Question Within a Question

Bennie paused to catch his breath after the steep climb up the steps to the terrace. He looked worriedly at O. P. and said, "We've been gone a long time."

"I doubt that we'll have even been missed," said O. P.

"You'd better be careful what you say when we get back in there," Bennie warned.

O. P.'s eyebrows rose quizzically. "Would you prefer to do the talking?"

"No," said Bennie quickly. "No, it's best that you do it."

"That's what I thought," O. P. dryly rejoined. "Why jeopardize two careers when one—mine—will suffice!"

Rapley was sitting at the kitchen table in his shirt-sleeves. Seated opposite him was the cook, Winifred Inch. Inch was standing at the head of the table looking at them.

"It's bound to come out now," said Mrs. Inch.

"Not necessarily," said Inch. "Not if we keep our heads. Why should it?"

"A sudden, unexpected death and a suicide, both within an hour of one another and in the same house?" Mrs. Inch slowly shook her head. "No, Inch," she said. "A lot of questions are going to be asked."

"Miss Cobb's death isn't likely to be classed as unexpected," he said. "You said yourself that you weren't surprised her heart had given out after that bronchial virus."

Winifred Inch looked at the chauffeur. "Well," she said, "you've not been having much to say for yourself. This concerns you too, you know. If we're out of a job, so are you."

Rapley said to Inch, "Nobody suspects anything about Faye Gould, do they?"

"I'm not sure," replied Inch. "That friend of Miss Cobb's . . . I didn't think she was entirely happy about things."

"What would she know?" said Rapley dismissively.

"We still haven't found out what she's really doing here," said Inch. "I think she's someone Midas knows—he invited her, not Miss Cobb. I'm pretty sure I'm not imagining things. . . . Every now and then they glance at one another as if they're sharing some kind of secret."

Rapley frowned. "You don't think—?"

"What is it?" asked Inch when he paused.

Rapley shrugged. "Never mind . . . I was just thinking out loud." He got up and put on his jacket which had been hanging on the back of his chair. He grinned. "You two worry too much. Midas isn't going to find out anything. Nor are the police. They never suspect the butler in real life," he added. "Everybody who can read knows that Danny Midas' butler is called Inch and that Inch and his wife have been with him for years and years. Who'd suspect the old and faithful family retainers?"

"But that isn't *us,*" Mrs. Inch interrupted. "Midas has called all his butlers Inch."

"Ah," said Rapley, going to the door, "but nobody but us and Midas knows that, do they? He's not likely to say anything, and neither are we. So like Inch said . . ." He grinned again and tapped the side of his nose with a forefinger. "When the cops come, keep your heads. Speak only when you're spoken to and don't have too much to say."

Winifred Inch listened to the creaking of the gate to the kitchen garden as Rapley opened and closed it.

"I've got one of my feelings," she announced abruptly. "Our luck has finally run out. I thought it was too good to last."

"No, don't be silly," said Inch. "Nobody's going to give us a second thought. Why should they? A thoroughly dull, respectable couple like us! Rapley is right there."

"If he is, it'll be the first time. He hasn't exactly shown himself to be too clever in the past, has he? In and out of Borstal, then prison. Lying, stealing . . ."

"That's his mother's fault for having been too soft with him."

"His mother's fault!" Mrs. Inch looked at Inch indignantly. "Her husband's, you mean."

Rapley paused in the rose garden and looked thoughtfully back at the towering black edifice behind him. He'd seen Danny Midas do some pretty strange things in his time, but tonight's little effort was going to take some beating. It had backfired on him, of course. Cobby konking out on him like that in the middle of his charade. Midas, he decided, was going off his head. Something had finally tipped him right over the edge. The show—something to do with that scene backstage at the theatre on Wednesday night during the first act. . . .

Rapley moved on, tried to remember exactly what Freda Cobb had said to him in the café that night. . . . Something about a note and Midas being killed. No, she said he was *going* to be killed. . . .

She'd been terrified out of her wits. And so had Midas, he recalled, remembering how he had rushed back to the theatre with Freda Cobb and found Midas semi-collapsed backstage. Cobby's heart had stood up to all the excitement that night remarkably well—under the circumstances. She had raced him back to the theatre, run like a hare! She'd been a peculiar old duck where Midas was concerned, though. . . . Absolutely terrified that something was going to happen to him. At least, thought Rapley, that was the impression she always gave him. And yet she had everything to gain by his death. Inch had overheard Midas telling her once that in the event of his death, everything—with the exception of a few charitable bequests—went to her.

He would imagine that their relationship was fairly typical of its type. The way he saw it, Midas and Cobby had stuck together through thick and thin because they were "family," not because they were particularly fond of one another. She'd had to know her place, though. It wasn't as if Midas actually ever said anything to her, but he never really let her forget that she was only an in-law living off his charity. And you could tell by the way she watched him sometimes, how she analysed his moods and that she was always very careful never to overstep the mark with him.

Odd, what Inch had said about Faye Gould. . . . That she thought Cobby was Midas' wife.

Now what, he wondered, could have given her that daft idea?

He crossed the cobbled yard to the garaging, unlocked the double door, and switched on the light. It had been years since horses were last stabled there, but he could still smell them, the hay. . . .

In the distance a dog barked furiously. Bruno . . . One of these nights that wily old fox was going to pick the vicious little swine up by the throat and shake the living daylights out of him. "If I don't get to him first," muttered Rapley.

Grinning to himself, he got into the estate car. Never mind the wishful thinking about running Bruno down . . . He'd better keep an eye out for Rosenberg and O. P. Charming if he ran them down!

Rapley's eyes suddenly narrowed. Inch hadn't said anything about him, O. P. . . . Whether O. P. had found the guest cottage and tumbled to Midas' little game with them.

Rapley thought for a minute. He'd forgotten all about that. . . .

His face thinned with concentration as he recalled his having followed O. P. as far as the swimming-pool. . . . More amusing then than important. But now he wondered. . . .

His mind moved quickly, trying to grasp the elusive thread of thought which one moment was very nearly within his reach and then, in the same instant, snatched away.

A tingle of excitement went through him. Then he smiled, even though he still couldn't quite pin down the thought so that he could examine it closely. Particularly since it was now being chased by a question within a question.

What if Freda Cobb didn't die of natural causes? What if she were murdered?

CHAPTER 10

Accusations Are Made

"I think," said O. P. to Danny Midas, "that the time has come for you to come clean and lay your cards on the table. Though knowing you, they'll all be faked—trick cards."

O. P. looked round at the tense, unsmiling faces of the five people who had returned with Danny Midas to the drawing-room to await the arrival of the police. Bruce Neville was in the study, deaf to Lilla's cajoling and coaxing to come and join them.

"We want some answers. Don't we, Bennie?" O. P. added, smiling to himself when Bennie frowned back at him and then stared mutely at the floor.

It suddenly occurred to O. P. that he was standing completely alone. He had not really expected Bennie to back him up, but he was a little puzzled that the others hadn't added their voices to his. At least one of them, anyway.

Danny Midas said, "As you wish. But first I think you should know that Faye is dead. She's shot herself with Bruce's gun."

Bennie looked quickly at O. P., who asked sharply, "When did this happen?"

Danny Midas shrugged. "Somebody—Cappy—went looking for Lilla and found Faye instead."

"Poor old Faye," said O. P. slowly. Then: "Where is she?"

"In the cloakroom at the other end of the hall—the toilet to be precise," said Danny Midas. "I've instructed Inch to lock up the cloakroom, and Rapley's gone to fetch the police."

O. P. looked round at everyone again. "Then all the more reason, I'd say, for all of us to get our stories straight."

"What do you mean?" asked Lilla.

"I mean that if Danny doesn't tell us why he's been playing cat and mouse with us all night, then he'll have to tell the police, who are surely going to think they've been called out to some kind of nut-house. . . . You know, when people start talking about dinner parties in a small cottage that's supposed to be Danny Midas' country mansion, Abracadabra, and isn't, and catering staff who are hired to turn up, and don't, and sabotaged fireworks displays, and minibuses that inexplicably disappear . . ."

"I think you've made your point," said Danny Midas coldly. He crossed to the bell-pull at the side of the fireplace and rang for the butler. Inch appeared almost as if he had been waiting outside the door for just such a summons. "Would you please fetch Mrs. Inch," Danny Midas said to him. "I wish to have a word with both of you."

Inch did not speak. He turned and went out, then Danny Midas asked Lilla if she wouldn't mind seeing if Bruce had finished blubbering, and if so, would she please request him to join them immediately.

When everyone had assembled, Danny Midas said, "I have gathered you all here tonight because I believe one of you is trying to kill me."

O. P. laughed. "Now I know you're mad!"

"Very well, then. The police will be here shortly. I'll present all the evidence to them, and we'll see what they have to say about it."

O. P. looked at him steadily. "You're serious about this, aren't you?"

Danny Midas did not reply.

O. P. considered him for a moment. Then, inclining his head at Mrs. Charles, he asked, "Does this mean she's one of your suspects too?"

"Mrs. Charles agreed to come here tonight to meet you—and observe how each of you would react under extremely stressful conditions—and then advise me which of you she thinks is involved in a plot to kill me."

"Good God," said O. P. softly. "He's called in a shrink!"

Danny Midas said coolly, "Mrs. Charles is perhaps better known as Madame Adele Herrmann, the clairvoyante. And I make no pretence about it; if it were not for the fact that my late sister-in-law, Miss Cobb, insisted on my asking Mrs. Charles's advice first, I would have informed the police days ago of the attempt which I suspect one of you contrived to have made on my life last Thursday night. If I'm wrong—and quite frankly, I don't think for one moment that I am—then you will all have my sincerest apologies for ever having suspected you, and I will look elsewhere for the would-be assassin—the person, or persons, my wife has hired to aid and abet her in disposing of me."

O. P. wasn't the only one who stared at him in disbelief. The Inches, however, looked more worried than disbelieving, though of them both, Inch was the more composed, frowning a quick warning at Mrs. Inch to be silent when it appeared that she was about to make some protest in their defence.

Bruce glared vengefully at Danny Midas. "You're just saying all this to torment us, make us feel guilty so you can get rid of us without anybody kicking up a fuss." Bruce's voice rose hysterically. "D'you think I don't know what you're up to? For years I've watched you get rid of people you no longer have any use for or you've suddenly grown tired of having around."

Bruce looked frantically round at the others. "He never fires anybody, you know—that's far too simple and straightforward for Danny Midas, nowhere near devious enough. He uses psychological tricks to get rid of them—wears people down so that in the finish, they leave him. No court cases for unfair dismissal, no awards of compensation, no redundancy payments . . ."

Bruce saw the quick look the Inches gave one another. Turning to Inch, he then went on:

"Didn't you ever wonder why he wasn't fussy about your lack of references? I daresay you thought he had a heart of gold to take the pair of you on the way he did, on face value only. Well, that's a laugh! Three years, that's the longest any of the household staff lasts around here, and then, *chip, chip!* Danny Midas starts chipping away at them until they run screaming from the place. They can't get away fast enough. By my reckoning that gives you about three months before he starts working on you. Never mind the poor old cow upstairs. . . . It would never have been her who stabbed you in the back. It's Danny Midas you've got to watch out for."

Danny Midas said quietly, "All finished, Bruce?"

"You're wicked and cruel, and I hate you. I wish you were dead!" cried Bruce, and wheeling round he fled from the room.

"You sure can pick 'em," murmured O. P., an observation to which Danny Midas reacted with an annoyed frown.

Lilla asked, "Wouldn't it have been simpler to arrange a meeting at the theatre and have this out with us there? I don't think it was necessary for us to be put through all this unpleasantness tonight. Frankly, I can't see the point of it."

"Oh, I don't know," drawled O. P. "If you ask me, the Fairy Queen summed it up pretty well, the way Danny operates. Well, chums"—he grinned—"don't ever say your Uncle O. P. didn't warn you. I told you Danny was paranoid."

"Yes, but not about us, surely," said Leo protestingly. He looked at Danny Midas. "I can't seriously believe that you would think, or have any reason to suspect, that one of us would want to harm you in any way. It's ludicrous . . ."

There was a knock on the door, and Rapley came in. Danny Midas looked at him, surprised. "That was quick. The police are on their way?"

"I haven't gone yet," said Rapley. "And I'm not about to go anywhere either. To fetch the police or anyone else." He looked slowly round the room at the others. Then, coming back to Danny Midas: "The rotor arms are missing from the cars—the Rolls and the Ford. Somebody's lifted them."

Cappy, who had been standing sullenly apart from the others, started forward. "What does that mean?"

"Exactly what he said," O. P. rejoined. He smiled faintly. "He ain't going nowhere—not in a car minus a rotor arm he isn't!"

Her eyes widened. "You can fix it, can't you?" she asked the chauffeur.

"Only if you give me back the rotor arms, miss," he replied.

She looked alarmed. "I haven't got them! I don't even know what they are. I know nothing about cars. I can't even drive one!"

There was a silence. Then Danny looked at Leo and said, "You were saying, Leo? Something, I think, about it being ludicrous for me to suspect that one of you would wish to see me dead? If the cut telephone wires didn't prove my point, then the missing rotor arms from my cars surely must. I can't say about the estate car, but the Rolls was definitely in perfect working order not two hours ago. It seems fairly elementary, wouldn't you say? that one of you —somebody here in this room—first put the telephone, our immediate link with the outside world, out of action, and then immobilized our only means of transport."

"Well, there's nothing wrong with my legs," said Bennie. "I'll walk into the village to get help."

"I'll just bet you would," said Teddy.

"What d'you mean by that crack?" Bennie demanded.

"I think," said O. P., "that what Teddy is really saying is that he doesn't trust you."

Bennie stared at O. P., then at Teddy, who said, "Don't you think you should tell us where you really went when you said you were going to phone your mother—the one we all know died five years ago?"

Cappy was looking at Bennie strangely. "I remember now. . . . When the butler said he'd show you the way to the library, you said not to bother."

Startled, Bennie exclaimed, "Yes, of course I said I knew where the library was! I'd seen the bus driver go in there to use the phone, hadn't I? We all had—"

Danny Midas looked at him sternly. "You cut the telephone wires, didn't you, Bennie?"

Bennie's head shot round, and he stared at him.

Danny Midas went on, "The changes in the show you've been wanting me to make—my wife put you up to that, didn't she?"

"No—*no!*" protested Bennie. "It isn't true! I admit I know that the show doesn't deal fairly with her, and that she's painted a lot blacker than she really was, but I discovered that through my own researches. I've never met her, I swear it! You wanted a shrew for a wife, I gave you one, did exactly what *you* wanted—all the way along the line. And those—the scenes with your wife in them— weren't what I wanted to change, anyway." He moistened his lips nervously, his voice cracked. "It's the last act that needs pruning, tightening up. It's too long-winded."

Rapley said, "I don't think it was Mr. Rosenberg who touched the cars. I think that was you, sir." He grinned at O. P., then turned to Danny Midas and explained: "After I'd finished garaging the Rolls, I spotted Mr. Oliver snooping about the grounds. I followed him as far as the swimming-pool, then it looked to me as if he was heading back my way, and as I didn't want him to see me, I turned round and went inside."

O. P. said nastily, "You'd better watch out, Bennie. There's someone who can actually tell a taller tale than you can!"

"I never touched those telephone wires," said Bennie stubbornly.

"I wasn't talking about that," said O. P. "I meant the show."

Leo said solemnly, "You're changing the subject, O. P. Let's see your hands."

O. P. gave him an odd look but held out his hands. Leo examined them on both sides. They were surprisingly dirty, though there were no apparent signs of engine grease (if that were what Leo had hoped to find). O. P.'s eyes smiled mockingly into Leo's as the latter raised his head, then O. P. fell on his knees before Danny Midas and said, "Don't beat me, Kind Sir. I did it, I confess! It's the drink. I can't help myself."

Danny Midas snapped, "Well, where are they?"

O. P. looked up at him. "Oh," he said and frowned. He looked back at Rapley. "I don't suppose you happened to notice what I did with them—the rotor arms—while you were sneaking about spying on me?"

Cappy said, "Oh, for heaven's sake, get up, O. P. You're not funny."

O. P. scrambled grinning to his feet. "I do hope that this, the long, pointing finger of suspicion, means that I can't be trusted either and that somebody else will get the pleasure of walking into the village—or town—for help."

Nobody said anything.

"Why don't we all go?" he suggested brightly.

"The only place I'm going is home," said Cappy.

"I doubt that I could walk anywhere even if I wanted to," said Lilla, her injured leg stretched out in front of her.

Cappy eyed Rapley distrustfully. "Shouldn't someone go out and check that the rotor thingees really have disappeared?" She looked at Danny Midas antagonistically. "How can you be so damned sure that it isn't Rapley who wants to get rid of you and that he hasn't messed about with the cars so he couldn't go and get the police?"

"I think the young lady might've overheard our conversation the other evening at the theatre, sir," said Rapley with a sly smile. "She might've mistaken our little talk for a threat of dismissal."

"Nonsense," said Danny Midas. "There was and is no question of your being fired."

"No, of course not, sir," said Rapley, flashing a malicious glance at Cappy. "But the young lady mightn't necessarily have realized that, might she?"

"I've no idea what you're talking about, either of you," she said archly. "I'm not in the habit of listening at doors."

O. P. let out a derisive hoot, and she gave him an explosive look.

Teddy said, "I think Cappy's right. Somebody should check that Rapley's telling the truth. Who knows"—he looked first at Leo, then at Ray—"Danny might've put him up to it."

"I like it, I *like* it!" said O. P., rubbing his hands together.

Teddy said, "I'll go with Rapley and check that the cars are genuinely out of action."

O. P. held up his hands. "*Whoa!* Hold everything right there! How do we know that you and Rapley aren't in this together? There's still the little matter of your lengthy disappearance earlier when nobody knew where you were."

Teddy's eyes widened protestingly. "I was in the study with Bruce. You know I was. Ask Bruce."

"Ah," said O. P., smiling faintly. "In other words, Bruce will vouch for you and—correct me if I'm wrong—you will then turn round and vouch for Bruce."

Teddy's face hardened. "What are you driving at?"

"Maybe I've got it all wrong about you and Rapley," said O. P. Teddy stared at him.

Ray said, "I'd offer to go with Rapley only I suspect that O. P. would then remind us all that I too was missing for a time. . . . While I was looking for you, Teddy," he explained. He paused and looked at the butler and the cook. "And as for Mr. and Mrs. Inch here—well, nobody but they themselves know what they've been doing all evening."

O. P. smiled. "My word, aren't we having fun!"

Cappy snarled, "You've got a lousy sense of humour!"

Ray continued, "So really that only leaves the ladies, Lilla, Cappy, or Mrs. Charles—"

Lilla said, "I'll take Rapley's word for it. I wouldn't know a rotor arm if I fell over one."

"The same goes for me," said Cappy quickly.

"And me, I'm afraid," said the clairvoyante.

"Right then," said O. P. "Now we're getting somewhere. Rapley's story can't be checked out because (a) nobody can be trusted for one reason or another—whether it be because of a conspiracy with some other person (Rapley and Bruce being, for my money, the most likely co-conspirators at this point), or (b) because of a lack of familiarity with the engine of a motor car. Neither can anybody be trusted to go and fetch the police on foot. Other than the ladies, of course—one of whom is incapable of walking any great distance, another refuses, and the third—"

O. P. paused and looked thoughtfully at Mrs. Charles. "With all due respect, dear lady, with the passing of every moment, I confess to becoming increasingly suspicious of you. You can't deny that you, Danny, and Miss Cobb were in league with one another, and I now find myself wondering if it isn't a conspiracy that goes a whole lot deeper than that. Danny assures us that one of us is conspiring with his wife to kill him, but I can't help asking myself if it wasn't his sister-in-law all along. . . . The strain and the suspense finally getting to her and killing her off first."

O. P. grinned. "Makes sense, you know. The supposedly meek and mild sister-in-law and the wife bringing in a clairvoyante to confuse the issue and cover up their dirty tracks. All for a big, fat fee, of course . . ."

Mrs. Charles smiled, made no comment.

"Well, at least you could trot out some of the psyche-scientific claptrap you lot go in for these days and deny it," said O. P., a trifle testily.

The clairvoyante slowly shook her head. "No, Mr. Oliver. I don't propose to deny anything. You see, you could be right."

He stared at her.

Danny Midas intervened. "This is getting us nowhere. It's very late, and I don't know about anybody else, but I'm tired. Arrangements were made several days ago for a coach to be here at eight-thirty in the morning to collect you and return you all to London. I think we can all be agreed that the driver—who may or may not be the one you had before—is above suspicion?"

He cast his eyes about the room, inviting any objection, and after a slightly hesitant look at the others, Leo said, "Yes," and the rest nodded.

"Very well, then," said Danny Midas. "We will send *him* for the police. Now"—he went on—"in the meanwhile, I suggest we try and get some rest." He turned to Inch. "Would you and Mrs. Inch please show my guests to their rooms."

"Would you believe it?" murmured O. P. "He had it all worked out. . . ."

Danny Midas heard the remark but ignored it. He looked at Rapley. "As Inch will be tied up for a while, perhaps you should see to it that Bruno's locked up indoors. I don't want him barking all night," he said with an irritable frown. "I'd suggest that you should look for him somewhere near the wood. He's looking for that old dog fox again."

"I was going to suggest that myself, sir," said Rapley.

Inch said, "It might be better if I went, sir. Rapley and Bruno don't seem to get along too well lately."

Danny Midas shrugged. "Suit yourself. Just so long as someone shuts him up. That dog's incessant yapping gets on my nerves."

Something covert passed between Inch and Rapley—a look, a slightly raised eyebrow—and the clairvoyante, seeing the exchange, wondered what it meant. She held back as the others went out with Danny Midas and the Inches into the hall and then proceeded up the stairs. Leo and O. P., who straggled a little behind the rest, paused at the top of the staircase and glanced down at her as she came out of the drawing-room. Leo said something to O. P. and then Danny Midas called to them to hurry up. Glancing again at her, they moved on.

Rapley had gone out to the kitchen, and after pausing in the hall for a few moments, Mrs. Charles followed him. He looked round sharply as she entered the room.

"I'm sorry if I startled you," she said.

He looked at her warily.

"I wonder if you could help me—Mr. Rapley, isn't it?" she asked pleasantly.

"That's right," he said. "Inch will be back in a moment."

"No, it's you I really wanted to talk to."

The chauffeur became even more wary. "What about?" he asked.

"Your employer, Mr. Midas." Mrs. Charles watched Rapley's face close up. "Oh, I'm quite sure he wouldn't object," she assured him. "In fact it's why I'm here, to ask questions. And observe," she added after a slight pause.

Rapley said nothing.

"Did Mr. Midas tell you about the attempt that was made on his life, or was it Miss Cobb?"

Rapley seemed surprised by the question. Then the wariness returned, and he frowned. "I only know what happened at the theatre the other night. I don't know anything about any attempt on his life. Mr. Midas isn't one to discuss his private business with his employees."

"What happened at the theatre?"

He jerked his head in the general direction of Freda Cobb's bedroom. "Didn't she tell you?"

"No," replied Mrs. Charles.

He thought for a moment, then shrugged. "Mr. Midas took her —Miss Cobb—to see the show (she couldn't be there opening night because of a bad chest infection, she was still getting over it), but he was really checking up on Mr. Rosenberg—making sure he hadn't monkeyed about with any of the dialogue. Mr. Midas is at the show most nights checking up, only those poor suckers"—he inclined his head at the hall—"don't know it. Anyway, on Wednesday night—the night Miss Cobb was there—Mr. Midas spotted a couple of small changes in the first act, and he was hopping mad about it. I wasn't there, of course," the chauffeur put in quickly. "I was round the corner in a café drinking tea to pass the time." He shrugged again. "And I'm really only guessing about what happened, putting two and two together like from what herself—her ladyship upstairs—said when she came to fetch me, and what I could figure out when I got to the theatre a few minutes later to collect Mr. Midas. . . ."

"Go on," said the clairvoyante when he paused.

"Well, the way I understand it, Mr. Midas and Miss Cobb left the main auditorium—during the first act, this was. Mr. Midas was in a rage about the changes Mr. Rosenberg had made, and he was going backstage to talk to the cast between acts and tell them to go back to the original version. But as he and Miss Cobb were coming out of the foyer to go round backstage, someone—one of these punk rockers with spiky dyed hair and a safety pin through his nose—suddenly stepped up to Mr. Midas and asked him if he was Danny Midas. Mr. Midas said he was, and then the lad said, ' 'Ere, this is for you then, guv,' or something like that—and stuffed a letter inside Mr. Midas' coat. Mr. Midas opened it and read it and came over so funny-peculiar that Miss Cobb thought he was going to have a seizure and snuff it. She managed somehow to get him round to the stage door and inside the theatre, then she left him with Charlie—the old boy on the door—and came and fetched me."

"Do you know what was in the letter?"

The chauffeur shook his head. "Mr. Midas never said . . . I never even saw it. I only know there was a letter—or a note (something of the sort)—because of a couple of things I heard Cobby—Miss Cobb—say to Mr. Midas before we took off. I told you, I'm only guessing. . . ."

"Is that why you didn't seem surprised when you heard—for the first time tonight, if I am to understand you correctly—that someone has been threatening Mr. Midas' life?"

The clairvoyante, seeing Rapley hesitate, said, "But you were surprised, weren't you? even though you didn't show it. I think you thought he was being blackmailed."

"It's crossed my mind," he admitted. "Y'know . . . That note he got—well, he gets some pretty weird mail, I can tell you." He hesitated again and then, before he could stop himself: "But . . . well"—he shrugged—"you could never tell with those two."

"Oh? What do you mean?"

"I—" Rapley broke off, the sullen frown on his face betraying his regret at his unguarded comment. Then, with a small shrug: "When it came to pork pies, it was a close-run thing as to which of them was better at it."

"Pork pies?" The clairvoyante's eyebrows rose. "Lies, you mean?"

He remained silent.

"There was no letter, no punk rocker—the peculiar turn Mr. Midas had at the theatre was an act?"

A tiny, somehow furtive smile twitched at Rapley's thin lips.

"But why?" asked Mrs. Charles.

"That's Danny Midas, isn't it? The way he is . . . As my dear old mother would say, 'Full of the drama!' "

Quite true, thought Mrs. Charles a few minutes later as she left the kitchen and then walked round the stairs and into the hall. Danny Midas wouldn't be half the illusionist he was if he hadn't known, first and foremost, how to make the most of the stagecraft of the dramatic actor.

Mrs. Charles paused at the study door, knocked softly on it. When there was no answer, she quietly opened it and looked in, half expecting to see Bruce hunched in despair over the desk but finding instead the room in darkness and empty.

Switching on the light, she went in, quietly closing the door behind her.

CHAPTER 11

Lilla Tells Her History

Lilla was coming away from the bathroom when Mrs. Charles finally made her way quietly along the gloomy, gallerylike passage to her room. Unaware of the other woman's presence, Lilla abruptly paused and leaned heavily against the wood-panelled wall, lowered her head and closed her eyes. She looked extremely tired and in some considerable pain. She raised her head sharply when the clairvoyante spoke, smiling ruefully at the latter's concerned inquiry as to whether she could be of assistance.

"Ah," said Lilla. "Caught in the act!" She held out her arm for Mrs. Charles to take. "It's at times like this that one realizes just how old one is getting!"

Mrs. Charles helped her into her room.

"A chair, I think," said Lilla, indicating a large leather armchair over against the wall. "I'm not going to even attempt to lie down on the bed. This knee of mine is going to throb all night."

Mrs. Charles got a blanket from the bed and wrapped it around Lilla's legs.

"It's not so much the cut," said Lilla. "It was a reasonably clean, straightforward one. It's more my arthritis, I would think."

Mrs. Charles sat on the edge of the bed contemplating her. She was becoming increasingly conscious of her lack of an ally, someone whom she could talk to, trust, and of everyone, Lilla seemed the one most likely to fill that need. With possibly Leo Polomka and Ray Newman a close joint second. There had been very little time to draw any definite conclusions about anyone, other than that they were all inclined to be selfish and rather self-centred, but these three, to her mind, appeared the more stable in temperament.

Lilla was smiling at the clairvoyante. "You must think we're all quite mad. Danny Midas for certain . . . I've thought that myself for days—that he's been slowly going mad. But then"—she made an expressive gesture with her hand—"I daresay anyone would start acting a bit odd if they really believed somebody was trying to kill them."

"You seem doubtful."

"That someone's out to get Danny?" Lilla made a face. "As far as I'm concerned, he lost his grip on reality years ago. I've known him a long time, you know," she added with a solemn smile.

Mrs. Charles nodded. "Yes, I gathered as much."

Lilla was quiet for a few moments, reflective. Then she said, "Danny and I once came close to making a terrible mistake: we very nearly got married—back in our mad, mad youth, of course." She smiled wistfully. "He used to say he was only marrying me for my red hair, but actually it was for my father." She laughed at the quizzical expression on Mrs. Charles's face. "My father," she explained, "was an illusionist, a terrible performer—quite pathetic, in fact—but a brilliant ideas man and a great innovator."

Lilla laid her head back against the chair and closed her eyes. "Danny used to be one of those people who believe there's a magic key to the universe: find that key, and you had the answers to all the questions you'd ever need to ask. It took him a long time to find out that there isn't one, and that the secret he searched for and expected to find in others, people like my father, was within himself all the time."

"Yes, I know," said the clairvoyante quietly.

Lilla looked at her searchingly. "I thought that was strange. . . . When Danny said, or rather implied, that you and his sister-in-law were on intimate terms with one another. She looked the type who'd be scared to death of her own shadow. I couldn't imagine her having any close friends or acquaintances. I'd even go so far as to say she never put a foot outside this place without Danny's say-so."

Mrs. Charles said, "I met Miss Cobb for the first time this weekend." She paused. Then: "Had you met her before?"

Lilla shook her head. "No. Nor his wife. After Danny and I parted company, we completely lost touch until we met up again in Las Vegas early last year. I married about eighteen months after we broke up. . . . Somebody else," she added dryly, "who married me for my father, only this time round, the love of my life was a little more clever at concealing his real motives. Then when he'd got what he wanted from my poor old dad, picked his brains clean, he shook the dust of both of us off his feet and moved on to bigger and better things. Made quite a name for himself. And the irony of it now is that Danny Midas wants him. Isn't that a delicious twist of fate—the two men who went after me for my father's know-how finishing up working hand in glove?" Her cheerful grin faded. "I used to be quite pretty, you know. Even prettier than Cappy. Slimmer too . . ." She laughed, suddenly cheerful again.

"Is that her real name?" asked Mrs. Charles.

"Cappy?" Lilla thought for a moment, then shook her head. "I was just trying to remember it. I heard someone call her once by another name—not here, in America, I think—but I've forgotten what it was. She's called Cappy because she always wears her boyfriend's baseball cap when she's working—going through the routines with her dancers. He's a pitcher. Or maybe it's a catcher. . . ." She frowned. "Some such thing. I'm not really into baseball."

"Would you know if Danny's wife had red hair too?"

Lilla narrowed her eyes. "No, I wouldn't. I only know that people said she was a real stunner to look at. . . . Like the girl in the photograph downstairs. That's what made me think it might be her."

"Would any of the others know the colour of her hair?"

"Ray might—Ray Newman. But why not ask Danny?" Lilla frowned quickly. "No, that wouldn't be very tactful, would it? Not in the circumstances . . . I mean, if—" She broke off, eyed the clairvoyante shrewdly.

"What is it?"

"You're not thinking that Cappy's mixed up in this plot Danny was talking about a while ago?"

Mrs. Charles smiled and shook her head. "No, not really. It was just a thought that crossed my mind—that Mrs. Midas might've had a child, a daughter."

Lilla pondered the possibility. "I daresay she could have—why not?" She spoke slowly, in step with her thoughts. "I'm not really sure of Cappy's age. . . . Jo Midas' daughter, eh? Now there's a thought to conjure with, if you'll pardon the pun!"

"You know Cappy, you've worked with her. What do you think?"

"My dear," said Lilla heavily, "I think that in our profession, anything is possible. But that—well, that . . . thinking Cappy might be Jo Midas' daughter—is carrying things a little too far. Though I'll admit that in many ways she's very like Danny—if that's another possibility you're considering, that he's her father. They've both got that same ruthless streak, the relentless drive and total selfish lack of consideration for others. But no . . ." Lilla shook her head. "I'll eat my wig if she's his daughter. Or his wife's by some other man. You've got hold of a proper red herring there," she laughed.

"Yes, probably," agreed Mrs. Charles, thoughtfully eyeing Lilla's hair and deciding that it was indeed a wig.

"And she's not mine either," said Lilla with a wry smile. "If that's what that busy little mind of yours is wondering now! Don't let this fool you." She yanked off her wig and tossed it on the bed, then massaged her patchy scalp with her fingertips. "Sure my hair was red when I was young, but not Cappy's colour. Nowhere near as dark, more reddish gold. Much prettier, softer—even if I say so myself." She gazed at the clairvoyante's feathery, pale gold hair, sighed. "Y'know something? Growing old is a real pain. I hate it. My mother went bald like this—only temporarily. Alopecia areata, they called it. . . . Brought on by the shock of my father's death, they said." She grinned a little. "Got that all wrong, didn't they? As a kid I always thought there was something peculiar about my old gran's hair, and now I'm pretty sure I know what it was. She went bald like this too and had to wear a wig. Ah well . . ." She grinned again. "I always wanted to be different."

She hesitated. Then: "But harking back to Cappy . . . I don't profess to be much of a student of human nature, but I do know one thing about her. If she were in any way involved in a conspiracy against Danny Midas, she'd have blown her cover—as they say —ages ago. The very first time Danny crossed her and she lost her temper, she would've told all, she wouldn't have been able to stop herself. When she gets mad with someone, her tongue literally runs away with her. Probably something like once or twice in any given day, she'll express a desire to kill Danny. But then so will I. And Bennie. And any number of other people I could mention. . . . The exception being Leo Polomka who would cut out his tongue and hope to die if he ever said a cruel harsh word against anybody!"

"About Bennie," said Mrs. Charles.

"What Teddy said about his mother?" guessed Lilla. She made a dismissive gesture. "There are some people who develop psychosomatic illnesses—a stomach-ache or maybe it'll be a headache—to get them out of an unpleasant situation. . . . When Bennie has to do something he doesn't want to do, or he wants to get out of something, he suffers an acute attack of motheritis. His problem is that he's never learned how to stand up on his own two feet and say no. O. P.'s every bit as bad. He hides behind a drink problem. At least, that's the way it looks to me." She shrugged. "Still, I suppose everybody does a little of that sort of thing. We've all got our own means of covering up our inadequacies, haven't we?"

"Including Danny Midas?"

Lilla smiled. "Specially Danny Midas. He's the grand-daddy of them all when it comes to that game. His basic inadequacy is his fear that he won't get what he wants. He plays one person off against another—clever psychology, you may think. . . . Engender just the right amount of anxiety, and up goes the performance level. And it's true that some of the time, that is what he's doing. But not always. Often this is nothing more than a cover-up. He's really getting ready to give them both the push and swing in a third person—the real object of his desires. And the other two rabbits, who have been so obsessed with themselves and each other, don't know what's hit them. By then it's too late for them to do anything about it, anyway. They've been outmanoeuvred and left high and dry! And the funny thing about it is that everybody knows what Danny's like, how devious he can be, and yet he still catches everyone out. They can't see when it's happening to them. And the smarter you think you are—like O. P.—the harder you usually end up falling."

"Haven't I seen his name, Oliver, listed in the credits for Danny's TV show?"

Lilla nodded. "O. P.'s brother, Denis, is Danny's TV producer." She hesitated. Then: "Have you known Danny long?" She laughed lightly. "I've an idea we might be two of a kind. . . . You're one of his old flames too, aren't you? He always did have a powerful strong weakness for the blondes and redheads, did our Danny!"

Mrs. Charles smiled. "That key you were talking about a few minutes ago—the one you said he was always looking for. . . . He asked me once if I thought he would ever be a big name." The clairvoyante smiled again. "Needless to say, we were both very young at the time."

"And?" asked Lilla when Mrs. Charles paused.

"I think I laughed at him."

"Oh dear," said Lilla and smiled. "Danny wouldn't have liked that—your not taking him seriously. He can't bear that." Her eyes narrowed. "So what about now? Are you still laughing at him?"

"No, this time I'm taking him quite seriously."

Lilla inclined her head to one side and studied the other woman meditatively. "People don't usually get a second chance with Danny."

Mrs. Charles smiled. "I think you might be like O. P. and looking for something that isn't actually there or, if it is, is of no real consequence."

They were quiet for a moment. Then Lilla asked, "Do you think Danny was telling the truth about wanting to go to the police about this so-called plot against him?"

Mrs. Charles considered the question. "Yes, I think so," she said at length. "I don't doubt for one moment that he would've contacted the police about the threat to his life, as he claimed, if it hadn't been for his sister-in-law's insistence (for reasons known only to herself) that he didn't involve them. Perhaps it pleased him to humour her. . . ." She hesitated, frowned. "I'm not really sure why he did things her way. I understand that she read a newspaper article about me and the assistance I've given the police on a number of occasions with their investigations into unusual crimes, and when she drew Danny's attention to it, he told her he knew me slightly. Everything followed on from there."

Lilla looked at her contemplatively. "You didn't know Miss Cobb was going to have a heart attack and die, did you? I don't mean to be rude," she said quickly, "but why was that? Shouldn't she have been giving off some sort of aura that you as a clairvoyante could see?"

"The only aura emanating from Miss Cobb was one of fear, and there's nothing subtle about real fear, Miss Osborne. It overwhelms and overpowers every other emotion, blocks out everything else."

Lilla considered the clairvoyante's explanation. Rather a glib one, she thought, but interesting none the less.

"Miss Cobb must've been very fond of Danny to have been that afraid for him."

"*Of* him," Mrs. Charles quietly corrected her. "An observation which Mrs. Gould made to me while we were alone together in the library was, I think, basically correct. Miss Cobb was very afraid of him. But my feeling was that it was a controlled kind of fear, something she—like many other people who come into direct contact with him—could cope with. I think she had a much stronger fear, the fear she had of herself. She didn't know how far she could trust herself, whether she was really completely under her own emotional self-control. She wanted desperately to tell me something tonight—maybe even make a confession, I'm not sure which—while at the same time being terrified witless that she would take me into her confidence."

There was a small silence. Then Lilla asked, "Have you told Danny any of this?"

Mrs. Charles shook her head. "No, not yet. In the morning, perhaps. We'll have to see. . . ."

Lilla narrowed her eyes thoughtfully at her. "You don't suppose Faye was right? She—Miss Cobb—was Danny's wife and that photograph downstairs in the study is only there to throw everyone off the scent. For reasons," Lilla interpolated in a grim aside, "only the convoluted mind of Danny Midas would know or understand." She was quiet for a minute, thinking. Then, shaking her head firmly: "No, she wasn't his wife. One look at this place tells you that. I'll bet you anything you like that Danny bought this house lock, stock, and barrel exactly as we see it tonight. With the exception of his study, of course. A wife would've changed things—those God-awful paintings hanging out there in the passage and down the stairs. Brightened the place up. Danny—like most men—wouldn't know where or how to begin, wouldn't have the time. Bruce could probably make something of the place, but then Danny isn't the type to give that sort of *carte blanche* to someone like him."

"How well do you know Bruce?"

Lilla shrugged a little. "I'd never met him till I came back home to do the show for Danny. He wasn't with Danny in America—Las Vegas. But I'd heard all about him, of course. . . . The accident. You know about that, I suppose." Then, when the clairvoyante shook her head: "Bruce used to be in the business—a professional

magician. It was a double act. Bruce's boy-friend Bobby—they
lived together—was the other half. Bobby performed all the
magic, Bruce really only walked on and off stage with the props,
generally assisted Bobby, and took care of the big cats—the two
female tigers they used in their opening and closing illusions.
Anyway"—she sighed—"Danny got them work in the States
through a contact of his, but at the last minute—just before they
were due to fly out to do the show—one of the cats developed an
abscess under one of its teeth which required surgery. Then when
it was taken away to be treated, the other cat got so mopey and
difficult to handle that it was finally decided that Bruce should stay
behind and take care of the animals and that Bobby would make
the trip on his own. Both Bruce and Bobby had wanted to cancel,
but Danny talked Bobby out of it."

Lilla paused, frowned. "I don't know exactly how it happened—
what went wrong—but during the first rehearsal with the tigers
that some animal trainer friend of Danny's in the States had
agreed to hire to Bobby, one of the cats attacked him, and he was
badly mauled. He died on his way to hospital."

"When did this happen?"

"Some years ago now. Bruce went completely to pieces over it
and spent a year in a mental home having psychiatric treatment.
Then when he came out, Danny was waiting for him with the offer
of a job. Out of the jaws of one man-eating tiger, you might say,"
Lilla added ruefully, "into the jaws of another. Bruce should really—"

She broke off as a loud explosion suddenly ripped through the
stillness of the night.

"What was that?" she asked quickly.

Mrs. Charles rose from the bed and crossed to the window, drew
aside the curtain. The window was spotted with raindrops.

"Can you see anything?" asked Lilla.

"No. It's too dark."

"It sounded like a car backfiring. Maybe Rapley fixed one of the
cars after all."

"I think I'll go down and see," said Mrs. Charles, going to the
door.

Lilla threw back the blanket and struggled to her feet. "Wait for me . . . I'm not staying here on my own. This place is beginning to give me the creeps. *Damn!*" she said abruptly and turned back to get her wig.

CHAPTER 12

The Question Is: What Did the Butler Find?

Mrs. Charles stood quietly at the stairhead. Seconds before, as she came along the passage, she thought she had heard a door below softly open and close.

The lights downstairs had been switched off, but she thought she could see someone moving about in the hall, a tall, thin shadow near the front door.

The hall lights suddenly came on.

Inch.

He was wearing a long black mackintosh and a grey knitted woolen cap. The Grim Reaper, thought the clairvoyante uneasily, taking in his gaunt, hollow-eyed look, the sallowness of his complexion.

He looked up quickly as Mrs. Charles started down the stairs.

"I heard a noise," she said. "An explosion of some kind. Somewhere outside, I thought."

"Yes, madam," said Inch. He was a little out of breath and, now that she was up close to him, even more cadaverous-looking in his black rainwear. "I was just about to take a look around outside," he added.

It was a stupid lie. His mackintosh, on its right upper arm and across part of the shoulder, was smeared with water, as if it had brushed against some wet shrubbery or the branch of a tree, and his shoes were damp and muddy. The sound she had heard of a door opening and closing had obviously been Inch returning to the house.

In the distance a dog began to bark excitedly. Inch turned his head to one side and listened to it, frowned.

"Miss Cobb's dog?" inquired Mrs. Charles.

"I would imagine so, madam," replied Inch. "Rapley must've had trouble finding him. Bruno can be as crafty as a fox when the mood takes him. If you'll excuse me, madam, I think it best if I go out and see to him before he disturbs Mr. Midas."

Inch went to the front door, opened it, and disappeared. Mrs. Charles waited a moment and then followed him as far as the door, opening it a fraction and looking out.

Inch was standing quite motionless on the terrace about twenty-five yards away, gazing in the direction of the wood. There was something about his stance which, to the clairvoyante's mind, suggested an attitude of utter helplessness. He knew what had caused the explosion—and his present interest in the wood, plus the mud on his shoes, indicated that this was where it had probably occurred—but he didn't know what to do about it, how best to proceed.

Mrs. Charles gently closed the door as he turned back.

She started a little when someone spoke her name.

Danny Midas.

He was doing up a mackintosh similar to the one Inch was wearing. On the hall table was a shotgun, a box of pellets, a large flashlight, and a pair of leather gloves.

Standing at the foot of the stairs was O. P. Bennie stood timorously at the head of them with Lilla. He was in shirt-sleeves. Curiously, his trousers were rolled up from the bottoms of the legs like a Mediterranean fisherman's, and he was barefoot. Mrs. Inch, in a thick blue tartan wool dressing-gown, her hair confined in a coarse white net, came round the back of the stairs and said harshly, "Inch?"

Danny Midas said, "I don't know where he is, Mrs. Inch. I'm just going to find out."

O. P. moved up to the hall table, looked at the shotgun. "Blimey," he said. "You don't mess about, do you?"

Mrs. Charles glanced down at his shoes which, like Inch's, were wet and muddy-looking, then she looked round thoughtfully at the front door. There was still no sign of the butler.

Bruce, wearing a white silk dressing-gown with a gold monogrammed pocket over matching pyjamas, joined Bennie and Lilla at the head of the stairs. He was grey-faced and haggard-looking. He spoke agitatedly, accusingly.

"That was a shotgun going off," he said.

Mrs. Inch started forward with a small cry. "Percy's not in his room. Inch went to find him."

"*Percy?*" drawled a sleepy voice, Cappy's. "Who the hell is Percy?"

She ran a hand through her tousled hair, started groggily down the stairs.

"Rapley," replied Danny Midas, loading the shotgun.

Cappy looked at him aghast, then turning to O. P., she said, "Where does he think he's going with that?"

"Butterfly hunting?" suggested O. P.

A door opened and closed, and a moment later Inch appeared. He came from the back of the house—through the kitchen, most probably.

Emotions which he had no doubt previously been able to hold in check were now given free rein. He was trembling, clearly distraught.

"What is it, Inch?" demanded Danny Midas.

"Rapley—" Inch drew himself up to his full six feet two inches, visibly got control of himself. "There's been a terrible accident."

Time stood absolutely still. Nobody said anything. Then Mrs. Inch threw herself at Inch, screaming abuse. Her strong hands were round his scraggy throat. "You always hated him. . . . Both of you," she screamed when Bruce came flying down the stairs to Inch's aid and wrested her away from him.

Mrs. Inch huddled against the wall, weeping. "I knew something was going to go wrong. We should never have done it," she sobbed. "It was wrong, wicked. . . ."

Danny Midas watched her for a moment, then turned to Inch, who had fallen back against the banister where Bruce was now ministering solicitously to him. "I've just been into the study. There was a shotgun missing from the gun cupboard."

Inch managed a weak nod. Bruce helped him to a carved wood settle and sat comfortingly beside him.

"Rapley took it with him when he went to fetch Bruno." Inch hunched over, and his lean frame shuddered. Bruce put an arm round him and patted his shoulder comfortingly. "He tripped over," Inch went on. "I couldn't tell for sure how it happened—it's so dark and wet out there. He must've fallen on the gun, and it went off." He lowered his head, his shoulders heaved.

Mrs. Inch stopped weeping. There was an expectant hush. Then, slowly, Inch raised his head and looked straight at Mrs. Inch who, when their eyes met, cried, *"Old poof!"* and then ran sobbing out to the kitchen.

Inch said brokenly, "He took the full blast in the chest. There was no hope, no hope." He shook his head dazedly.

Ray and Leo, who had been disturbed by Mrs. Inch's earlier outburst of screaming and had left their rooms to investigate, came slowly down the stairs. They were both fully dressed, Mrs. Charles noted as she slipped quietly past the stairs and then out to the kitchen.

Behind her, the men were discussing who would go with Danny Midas to the wood. . . . "To make sure," she could hear O. P. saying, "that Inch hasn't been at the cooking sherry."

She found Mrs. Inch sitting huddled at the kitchen table in much the same attitude of despair that Bruce had adopted in the study earlier that night.

There was an electric kettle on one of the work tops, and Mrs. Charles filled it with water, then searched around for the tea caddy and some cups and saucers.

Lilla, appearing in the doorway, nodded approvingly and sat down opposite Mrs. Inch. Bennie sidled into the room, quietly drew out a chair, and sat down. He had gone back to his room and put on his shoes and socks before coming downstairs again. He had also rolled down his trousers legs.

No one spoke. Then several minutes later, as Mrs. Charles was pouring the tea, Cappy came in and sat down. Pale and drawn, she acknowledged the tea Mrs. Charles set before her with a subdued nod.

"He was all I had," said Mrs. Inch all of a sudden.

Cappy looked vaguely alarmed, as if this, being face to face with a recently bereaved person were a new experience for her, and she did not know how to handle it, what to say. She frowned at her tea and then almost gladly—as though pleased to have found something to do—she picked up her cup and sipped determinedly from it.

Mrs. Inch said bitterly to Bennie, who looked up at her, startled, "They murdered him, you know. They killed my boy. Bruce and Inch, they planned it between them. Percy threatened to tell Mr. Midas about them, so they got rid of him." She looked round

beseechingly at Mrs. Charles. Her cheeks were wet with tears.
"Percy didn't mean it. He wouldn't have told on them—he
couldn't, not without hurting us, himself and me too. It was just
that he didn't want Bruce to take Inch away from us. That was
what Bruce said he was going to do. He said he had some money
put aside and that he was going to leave Mr. Midas, and he and
Inch were going into business together. They were going to open a
school for young men who wanted to train to be butlers, Bruce
said. And where would that have left Percy and me? Me with no
proper references, and Percy victimized and accused of all sorts of
things he never did at my last domestic post."

Fresh tears rolled slowly down her cheeks.

"We had an agreement, Inch and me. A gentleman's agreement,
he called it. He couldn't go back on that, could he?"

"Are you really so sure he meant to break his word to you?"
asked Mrs. Charles, and Lilla widened her eyes quizzically at
Cappy. The bemused expression on Cappy's face conveyed the
impression that she too was finding the conversation difficult to
follow.

"Sure enough," replied Mrs. Inch, fumbling in the pocket of her
dressing-gown for a handkerchief and then using it. "Three
years," she went on. "That wasn't long to ask him to wait off, was
it?"

Again Lilla and Cappy exchanged baffled looks.

"That's when you planned to retire?" guessed the clairvoyante,
and Mrs. Inch nodded. She went on:

"There was never nothing on paper, mind. . . . Like I said, it
was a gentleman's agreement we made in a little teashop round
the corner from the employment agency. You see"—she frowned
—"people today want couples—the man to do some butlering and
the odd job or two about the place, and the woman to cook and
housekeep. They're not interested in singles—a widow like me
with a headstrong young lad to bring up, or a man like Inch who'd
had trouble at his last post over his relationship with one of the
young under gardeners."

Mrs. Charles nodded. "So you and Mr. Inch decided to pose as a
respectable married couple."

"It was the only way we could both be sure of getting a decent
post, wasn't it?" said Mrs. Inch earnestly. "We were desperate.
Inch promised me he'd go straight—there'd be no more of the sort

of trouble he'd had before—and I promised I'd keep my boy out of mischief. I knew it was too good to last." She lowered her head onto her arms which were folded on the table. "I knew we'd get found out," she wept.

CHAPTER 13

Off with Their Heads!

The muted voices of the men returning from the wood suddenly filtered through from the hall, and a few moments later, Danny Midas, Ray, O. P., and Leo came into the kitchen.

Mrs. Inch raised her head from her arms and looked at Danny Midas defiantly. "I want the police," she declared. "I've got a statement to make." Then, frowning suspiciously: "Where are Inch and Bruce?"

"Inch has gone to rouse Teddy," Danny Midas replied, addressing himself more to Lilla than to the woman who had asked the question. "Bruce is getting dressed."

"Someone should've gone with those two to make sure they don't get away," said Mrs. Inch.

"Really, Mrs. Inch!" said Danny Midas irritably.

"I'm warning you," she said imperiously. "I'm holding you personally responsible for their escape. They were in it together. They killed my Percy."

"It was an accident, Mrs. Inch," said Danny Midas wearily. "Rapley tripped over the exposed root of a tree and fell on the shotgun, which unfortunately went off. You can see quite plainly where it all happened."

Lilla looked questioningly at O. P. who shrugged non-committally.

Leo said, "That's how it looked to me," which, for some reason the clairvoyante could not fathom, provoked a strange little smile from Lilla.

Lilla looked at Ray, and he nodded.

Mrs. Charles watched for some reaction from Lilla, but this time her features remained completely undisturbed.

The clairvoyante carried the image of Lilla's smile with her to the sink where she refilled the kettle to make fresh tea. It wasn't a pleased smile, nor was it the relieved smile of a co-conspirator, someone who had reason to hope for such a pronouncement from an independent, presumably trustworthy witness, Mrs. Charles decided as she plugged in the kettle. She looked round thoughtfully as Mrs. Inch said:

"Oh no . . ." The cook shook her head adamantly. "You're not going to make me believe that. Never! It was murder. Cold-blooded murder."

The clairvoyante set down fresh cups and saucers and added three more when Teddy, Bruce, and Inch came in.

Hatred twisted Mrs. Inch's face into a grotesque grimace. "You should be locked up," she snarled at Inch and Bruce. "Nobody's safe while you two are around. We'll all be killed in our beds before the night's out."

She glanced up quickly as the clairvoyante placed a restraining hand on her shoulder.

"But they killed him!" the cook protested.

"Very probably," said Mrs. Charles. "But this isn't the way to go about proving it, is it?"

Mrs. Inch stared at her. The clairvoyante had removed her hand from her shoulder, but Mrs. Inch could still feel it there restraining her. Or was it a warning to take care? The cook was suddenly doubtful, uneasy. "No," she mumbled, frowning. "You're right. I'm sorry."

Bruce stared at her for a moment, then looked frantically round the room at the others. "You don't believe that old witch, do you?" he asked Lilla. "She's only saying those things because she's jealous. She's always been jealous of me. She'd say and do anything to get me kicked out of my job. . . . Wouldn't she, Reggie?" he asked Inch.

Inch looked away, stared at the window.

"Reggie!" Bruce whined. "You can't do this to me, I can't bear it!" He looked round at everyone again. His eyes were wild and staring. "You all hate me, don't you? You're all jealous of me. You've all been looking for a chance to stick the boot in, and now you've got it!"

Lilla rose, took him firmly by the arm, made him sit down.

"Now shut up and behave yourself," she said, fixing him with a

steady look. "What Mrs. Charles has just said to Mrs. Inch goes for
you too. That sort of behaviour is hardly likely to convince anyone
of your innocence if you didn't kill Rapley, is it?"

"I didn't kill him," he said truculently.

"Good, I'm glad to hear it," she said, and sat down again.

Mrs. Inch said, "I think I'd like to go to my room and lie down for
a while."

Lilla said concernedly, "Would you like someone to go with
you?"

"No, I think I'd prefer to be on my own for a bit." Mrs. Inch rose
to her feet, looked at Danny Midas. "It's all going to come out now,
sir, and I think you'd better know—for when the police come. My
name's Rapley, same as Percy's, and I'm a widow. I'm sorry my
Percy and I lied to you, sir. Inch and me, we only did it—pretended that we were married and that Inch was my boy's stepfa-
ther—because we couldn't get a proper job." She paused, lowered
her gaze. "You won't want me to stay on now, I'll have my things
packed ready to leave first thing in the morning."

"That won't be necessary, Mrs. Inch," said Danny Midas. "We'll
talk again later—when you're feeling better."

She moved to the door. Then, pausing, she turned back to him
and said, "You are going to get the police?"—and more than one
person wondered at the tone of her voice, its curious rising inflec-
tion.

"Yes, Mrs. Inch," he replied. "At the first available opportunity.
You have my word on it."

She looked at him steadily, then abruptly nodded and went out.

"And when is that going to be, I wonder?" said O. P. as the door
closed behind her.

"Exactly how far is it to the nearest town?" asked Lilla.

"Thirty miles," replied Danny Midas. "That's by motorway. Farther if one uses the B roads. The coach will be here long before
anyone could walk that far."

"But there'd be houses here and there—like this one—along the
secondary roads, wouldn't there?" Lilla pointed out. "Whoever
went would surely be able to raise the alarm somewhere along the
way."

"Not necessarily," he said. "There's an open prison farm not far
from here, and local people are a bit chary about opening their
doors to strangers at night. A prisoner escaped a couple of months

ago and held a family hostage overnight, and it's made everyone very nervous and reluctant to let anyone inside their homes."

"But there'd be no need for that," she said. "Whoever went could simply shout through the door or a window to the people inside to phone the police." She frowned quite severely at him. "You really must do something about getting the police, you know. It's going to look very bad if you don't."

Bruce looked as if he were about to burst into tears. "Some friend you've turned out to be. Why bother with the police? Why not hold a kangaroo court? Then when you've reached your verdict about us, you can find a good strong tree and have yourselves a hanging party!"

Leo walked the length of the long narrow table and back again. Everyone else was now seated. They watched him in silence. Suddenly he paused and turned to face them. "I think Bruce has got something there. Why wash our dirty linen in public when we can do it in private?" He looked at Danny Midas, spoke calmly, firmly: "That's what will happen, you know, once the police are brought in. That is, if Mrs. Inch is going to make a fuss about young Rapley —and I think you would do well to accept the fact that she is. Have you thought about what it'll be like once the news media gets hold of what's been going on here tonight? And what if Mrs. Inch talks to the newspapers and keeps on insisting that it was murder? You'll be crucified, Danny."

Leo gazed slowly round at the intently thoughtful faces that were turned towards him. He went on:

"It's not often that I agree with what O. P. says, but there was one thing he said earlier tonight which, on reflection, I think makes good sense. We should talk this thing through between ourselves, sensibly, unemotionally—"

"You mean get our stories straight first," O. P. chipped in dryly, "before we talk to the boys in blue."

Leo looked at him for a moment. Then he said quietly, "I see no valid argument in favour of our publicly airing all our personal grievances with one another for the delectation and delight of the sensationalists. Do you really want Danny to tell the police that someone—one of us, his friends—is conspiring with his wife to kill him because of the show's harsh treatment of her?"

Leo looked earnestly at Danny Midas. "Is this really what *you* want? Have you honestly considered the consequences? If one of us—with the exception of you, of course, madam—," he said with a small bow to Mrs. Charles, "really is trying to kill Danny, then surely it shouldn't be too difficult to find out who that person is. And if, as Mrs. Inch insists, young Rapley's death was no accident, wouldn't it be likewise relatively simple for us to discover who the culprit or culprits are? The police don't have exclusive rights to all the brainpower, you know. We could have this mess sorted out between us in no time."

"Oh, charming," said Bruce, thin-lipped. "Let me save you the bother of measuring my neck. It's size fifteen."

Mrs. Charles glanced down the table at Lilla, who was still looking at Leo. The strange little smile which she had observed earlier was back in Lilla's eyes, on her lips.

O. P. said, "Well, I hate to be the one to throw a bucket of cold water on what should be a whole load of fun—that's if we take Leo's advice and hold our own court of inquiry—but aren't the police going to smell a rat? They're not completely daft, you know. They'll know it's a conspiracy."

"Of course they will," said Lilla with a dismissive wave of her hand. "The whole idea is ridiculous."

"I see nothing wrong with it," said Mrs. Charles meditatively. "Provided, however, that this is not merely a convenient diversion to conceal a murderer or murderers and that the conspiracy the police ultimately suspect is the right one."

Everyone stared at her. Then Bruce jumped up, pushed back his chair. "I'm not putting up with another minute of this." He pointed a trembling finger at Mrs. Charles. "How dare you talk about us like that? I'll have you up for defamation of character."

"Sit down and shut up," said O. P.

Bruce glowered at him but sat down again all the same. "Reggie and I," he muttered, "are the only victims of a conspiracy that I can see. She's got no right to say things like that."

"Wrong," said O. P. "That's why the good lady is here—to cast the evil eye over all of us. Right, Danny?"

Danny Midas nodded. "Yes. I'm afraid, Bruce—all of you—that what O. P. says is correct. Mrs. Charles has every right to look closely—as close as she likes—at all of us. And as your employer, Bruce, I instruct you to give her every assistance she requires."

Lilla, noting the rebellious look on Bruce's face, smiled, and said,

"Mrs. Charles isn't any ordinary clairvoyante, Bruce. She's worked with the police before."

Bruce looked at Mrs. Charles, then at Danny Midas, who said, "That's perfectly true. This is why my sister-in-law suggested seeking Mrs. Charles's advice before I went to the police with my suspicions."

"Now I've heard everything," said Cappy.

"I wouldn't scoff if I were you," said Lilla solemnly. She looked slowly round at the others, pausing finally when her gaze came to rest on Bruce and Inch. "If you, Bruce, or you, Mr. Inch, killed Rapley—if his death wasn't an accident, like Mrs. Inch says—then be assured that Mrs. Charles will find you out. Eventually . . . That is, if she hasn't already made up her mind about it, and I rather suspect that she has."

Bruce's eyes filled with tears. "I thought you were my friend, Lilla."

"It's because I am your friend, Bruce, that I'm advising you to co-operate with her," she said gently.

O. P. turned to her and said, "Excuse me. . . . But do I or do I not detect a certain smugness to your tone?"

Lilla smiled. "I admit that I could be a party to a conspiracy to kill Danny, but if Rapley was murdered, then I'm the one person Mrs. Charles knows is innocent of the crime. We were talking together in my room when we heard the shotgun go off."

"I was in the bathroom soaking my feet," said Bennie quickly. Everyone looked at him.

"A likely story," said O. P.

They started to argue among themselves as to their individual whereabouts when they either heard the shot which allegedly killed Rapley (as in the case of Danny Midas, O. P., Bennie, Bruce, and Cappy), or (in Ray and Leo's case) were disturbed by Mrs. Inch's screaming voice (Teddy claiming vehemently to have slept through all of it, a claim which Ray said he personally very much doubted).

As Mrs. Charles watched them, she had the unreal feeling of being in a theatre watching an extremely clever performance by some very skilled performers. Everyone said exactly the right thing at precisely the right moment, everyone made all the right gestures.

She let their voices fade and watched their performances as one would a mime. . . .

Bruce, one minute flushed and indignant, the next on the verge of tears. A neurotic, highly strung homosexual? Maybe. Then again, maybe not.

Bennie, threatening to take off his shoes and socks and show everyone his bunions—spineless, apparently accommodating to the point of compromising his own personal integrity, mother-fixated. Or was this merely the face he had elected to present for the occasion?

Cappy and O. P., hissing and snarling at one another (O. P. clearly in love with her, but it was highly doubtful that either one of them knew it). Rather a tiresome performance after a time. That is, if it were only an act.

Inch, the not-so-perfect butler, hollow-eyed and haunted-looking, content to remain silent and let Bruce handle their defence. Though the clairvoyante doubted that this would have been because Bruce was the better actor of the two. Inch's performance thus far (if he were indeed acting) had been superb, beautifully under-played.

Teddy, red-faced and perspiring, thumping the table when it would seem that it was Ray that he would dearly love to thump. Ray deliberately provoking him, highlighting the other man's weakness of character by visibly alerting Teddy's internal defence system to some threat of danger known possibly only to themselves. Lilla watching them, not saying anything but highly amused by their performance.

Leo . . . The strong, silent, thoughtful type. Ever the courteous gentleman. And yet, interestingly, the first to cast his vote in favour of a criminal complicity when the occasion called for it.

And finally, Danny Midas.

He had changed.

The Danny Midas she had known, while unashamedly nakedly ambitious, had been a nicer person. At least in those days, although it had not come easily to him, he had given all the appearances of trying to be nice, of wanting to be liked and accepted—perhaps even at times working a little too hard at it. She had never got to know him really well, but if she had been asked to give her impression of him in the early days, before he became the household name he was today, she would have said that underneath the brash exterior, there was a very sad and lonely young man waiting and wanting to be loved.

She realized that she had been completely wrong about him. This too had been part of the Danny Midas image, the clever illusion masking the ruthlessness behind his relentless climb to the top of his profession.

All pretence was now gone. He had no need of it any more. In his own little world he was a god, the supreme being who could say and do what he wanted and treat people just how he liked.

He was a cold, withdrawn, arrogant man—an extremely unlikable one—and she would not have been the least bit surprised if the entire creative team gathered there in the kitchen had conspired collectively to kill him. But she knew they hadn't, that if her suspicions were right and there was a much bigger conspiracy than the one to which she had been a willing party, then this was not it.

CHAPTER 14

Mock Court of Inquiry

Danny Midas' voice suddenly rose harshly above the rest, and the room fell silent. Everyone looked at him expectantly, waited. Then, turning to Mrs. Charles, he said:

"What you've just seen happen—indiscriminate arguing, bickering, bitter recriminations—is going to happen all over again, only more so, when the police eventually get here if something isn't sorted out between us beforehand. And the only way to do that is to hold our own court of inquiry, as has already been suggested—with you, the only independent party present, acting as adjudicator. What I propose is this: You call upon everyone individually to give his or her evidence, as would happen in a proper court trial—and with no one interrupting"—he looked round warningly at the others—"the person in the witness-box, so to speak. And then when you've heard what everyone has to say, you give us your findings which we"—he looked round again—"must agree to be bound by."

Leo said, "In other words, whatever Mrs. Charles comes up with at the end of all this is what we tell the police, and we stick to our story."

Bruce's mouth opened and then closed again firmly. There was no reaction from any of the others, and the clairvoyante wondered if it were this which had dissuaded him from making any further protest or whether he was simply conserving his energies for the next act.

"Well, what do you say?" Danny Midas asked her. "Will you agree?"

She looked at him for a moment. Then she said, "I'm not sure I understand what it is you really want me to do."

"Quite simply what you were asked to come here and do in the first place. I want to know who is behind the threats I've received." He smiled coldly. "Somewhere in this room is a Judas, and I want to know who that person is."

"And Rapley?" she asked.

"What about him?" he said impatiently. "His death was a straightforward accident. Mrs. Inch is a reasonably sensible woman. . . . Give her a few hours to recover from the shock of what has happened, and she'll be the first to agree that she was behaving hysterically."

"I see," said the clairvoyante. She looked slowly up and down the table. Then: "You all agree to this?"

"If that's what Danny wants and thinks is best," said Lilla with a shrug. "I'd personally rather that everything was kept on a civilized level than that we spend the next three or four hours while waiting for the coach to arrive fighting amongst ourselves like alley cats. That's not going to get us anywhere. However," she went on with the same strange little smile the clairvoyante had noticed before, "let me give you all fair warning. If any of you is hiding something, then beware. This lady"—she inclined her head at Mrs. Charles—"like I told Bruce, will find you out. She's no fool, take my word for it."

O. P. laughed softly. "He—or she—who protests, of course, immediately becoming suspect number one. No . . ." He shook his head. "We are not about to be caught out that way, are we, chums?"

There was a general murmur of assent, one or two people shook their heads.

"Very well," said Mrs. Charles. "I agree, but on two conditions. One, that I and I alone hear the evidence that is to be given by each individual person. . . ."

"I protest," said O. P. quickly.

"Me too," said Teddy.

"Yes, and it is for precisely that reason that I make the stipulation," said the clairvoyante. "Everything that's said will raise a protest from one person or another and that way nothing will be achieved."

"Mrs. Charles is right," said Lilla. "We might just as well forget about holding an investigation and fight it out to the death."

There was a small silence. Then O. P. said, "Okay. What's the second no-no?"

"The other condition concerns Rapley. Before we go any further, I would like to see his body."

Inch, who for the most part had been staring morosely at the window, looked round at her sharply. "No, madam," he said. "You can't."

Leo said, "I wouldn't advise it."

O. P. grinned at Mrs. Charles and then winked knowingly at Lilla. "Clever," he said.

"What is he talking about?" Bennie asked Lilla anxiously.

Lilla smiled and said, "O. P. doesn't think Mrs. Charles believes there is a body; he thinks she suspects that somebody—or maybe all of us—are having her on."

Bennie looked petrified. "I never said there was a body. I'm only taking his, their"—he jerked his head first at Danny Midas, then nodded in the general direction of Leo and Inch—"word for it."

Danny Midas looked annoyed. Curbing his irritation, he turned to Mrs. Charles and said, "As you wish. Though I fail to see any connection between Rapley's accident and what I've asked you to look into for me."

"I think we'd all better go along," said Mrs. Charles, rising.

"Not me," said Lilla flatly. "No way. I've had enough dead bodies for one night."

Cappy hesitated, then shook her head vehemently. "I couldn't . . ." she said. She looked at Danny Midas. "I'll stay with Lilla."

"No you won't, my girl," said Lilla. "I'm going up to bed. Alone. There's no point in my staying up if I'm not going to be allowed to listen in to your nasty little secrets. And you're not going to want to talk to me again, are you?" she asked Mrs. Charles.

The clairvoyante shook her head. "No, I don't think so." She turned to Cappy. "Perhaps you would prefer to check on Mrs. Inch and make sure that she's all right."

Cappy jumped up eagerly. "Where is her room?" she asked, and Inch gave her the directions. She hurried out before anyone could have second thoughts.

Everyone else went out into the hall where they paused and, after a small discussion about a lack in several instances of suitable outdoor clothing, decided to meet again at the front door in five minutes.

Lilla went back upstairs to her room, followed a few moments later by Mrs. Charles, who wanted to get a topcoat, and Bennie, who said he felt he ought to put on his jacket before going outside. At the head of the stairs, Mrs. Charles paused and looked down into the hall. Danny Midas was moving towards the front door with Leo, Ray, and Teddy. O. P. had disappeared into the drawing-room—looking for a drink, the clairvoyante suspected. Inch and Bruce stood alone in the middle of the hall like two lost sheep, not knowing which way to turn. Or, possibly, who their friends were, thought the clairvoyante.

Inch suddenly looked up and saw her watching them. Thoughtfully, she turned away.

She was conscious of the difference as soon as she opened the door and switched on the light.

At first she thought someone had been in there—Mrs. Inch, perhaps.

The clairvoyante looked to see if the bed had been turned back, but it hadn't been touched. Nor had any of the furniture been moved about—another thought which occurred to her. As far as she could remember, everything was exactly in the same place as before.

As she looked thoughtfully at each item in the room, Lilla's comment that Danny Midas had bought the mansion complete with furniture and fittings and altered nothing was struck home forcibly to her.

And yet the feeling persisted, that something about this room was different.

Suddenly she realized what it was. Its almost depressing similarity in all but one particular to the room next door, Miss Cobb's bedroom.

At the foot of the four-poster bed in Miss Cobb's room was an antique carved wood chest, the kind used to store bed-linen and blankets. The one in this, her guest's bedroom, stood not at the foot of the bed but squarely across the connecting door, effectively barring movement between the two rooms.

Mrs. Charles went up to the chest, which was nowhere near as old as the one in Miss Cobb's room and more functional in appearance, and gazed pensively at the connecting door. The key was in the lock, as Inch had said. Leaning over the chest, she unlocked the door, turned the handle. The door opened, as she had already observed, into Miss Cobb's room. She could only reach out and open the door wide enough to see the long, gloomy shadows cast along one wall by the low wattage night-light someone had left on. She could not see the bed at all.

Quietly, she closed the door and relocked it. She felt uneasy, as if she were again missing something, some more subtle but vitally important dissimilarity between the two rooms, which ought not to be overlooked.

Frowning, she turned away to get her coat, abruptly pausing as a curious feeling of *déjà vu* swept over her.

She turned, retraced her steps. And then she noticed something very peculiar, and slowly everything began to slot into place. She could see now why Freda Cobb might have gone to the connecting door. And it was not because she thought there was someone in the room beyond whom she could summon to her aid. It was not until *after* she had crossed to the connecting door that she had suffered her fatal heart attack. *And that made Freda Cobb an accessory to murder,* the clairvoyante realized with a sense of shock. *She had helped to commit the perfect crime. . . .*

Mrs. Charles stiffened, listened. There was someone in the passage outside her door. She waited, but there were no further sounds. But she knew the person was still there.

Quickly, she moved away from the connecting door, went over to the wardrobe, opened it, got out her coat, and slipped it on. She doubted that the door of her room had been quietly opened in those vital few seconds before she had become aware of someone's presence without; but if she were wrong, if someone had been secretly watching her through a crack in the door and seen what she was doing—or more importantly, where she was standing—then she knew there was every possibility that she would never leave that house alive.

Bennie looked up apprehensively as Mrs. Charles opened the door and stepped out into the passage.

"Oh, er," he said nervously. "I wasn't sure if you'd already gone down." He was puzzled by the expression on her face, dismissed the look she gave him as being only in his imagination. After all, why should she be afraid of him? She'd be the last person he'd ever think of harming. She reminded him too much of his mother for anything like that. . . . "I wonder if I might have a word with you in private?" he went on. "I mean in there." He nodded his head at her room. "Without the others knowing."

Behind his hesitant, conspiratorial smile the clairvoyante detected fear. Fear so great that his hands were actually shaking. She watched the beads of sweat crystallizing in the dimple in his pudgy chin and across his brow. Then before she could answer him, O. P. rounded the corner of the passage. He came to an abrupt halt when he saw them standing together, and a strange look crossed his face. Then he forced a smile.

"There you are. . . . We were beginning to get worried. Ready for the off, are we?"

Mrs. Charles glanced at Bennie, who gave her a frightened look and then scurried off towards O. P.

"Not trying to nobble the judge, were we?" O. P. asked him with a grin.

"Don't be ridiculous," said Bennie agitatedly. "Whatever gave you that idea?"

O. P. laughed easily, and they all went downstairs.

Rapley was wearing a long, shiny black mackintosh similar to the ones Danny Midas and Inch had on. Underneath the mackintosh, which was unfastened, he wore a white shirt. Thin black braces supported the grey trousers of his chauffeur's uniform. His hands were leather-gloved.

The front of his shirt had been blown away by the blast from the shotgun, as was most of his chest. Danny Midas, who had got down and rolled the body back a fraction so that Mrs. Charles and the silent, grave-faced men beside her could see the raw, red, bloody mess for themselves, looked up questioningly at the clairvoyante, who indicated with a small nod of her head that she had seen enough.

Danny Midas let the body fall back on top of the shotgun from which the fatal shot had been fired and straightened up. Then, gesturing to the other men to stand aside, he aimed the wide beam of his flashlight at the gnarled tree root which protruded from the soil not four feet from where Rapley lay. "You can see where he stubbed his toe," he said, going over to the root growth and shining the flashlight directly onto it. "There—where that small piece of bark has been chipped away."

"I've seen enough," mumbled Bennie, who was as white as a sheet. "I'm going back."

Without a word, everyone turned and followed him.

They regrouped in the hall. Danny Midas removed his mackintosh and handed it together with his gloves and the flashlight to Inch, who disappeared with them around the back of the stairs. Bruce, after hesitating briefly, went with him.

Turning to Mrs. Charles, Danny Midas said, "Well, what now? Who is going to be first?"

She looked round thoughtfully at the others. Then, coming back to him, she said, "You, I think."

His eyes rounded a little in surprise, then he shrugged and followed her into the drawing-room. The others went back to the kitchen to make some more tea and toast and to await their turn to be summoned.

CHAPTER 15

The Evidence of the Knave

Mrs. Charles and Danny Midas sat facing one another in comfortable leather armchairs.

He eyed her quizzically. "Well," he said. "Satisfied?"

"About Rapley?" She thought for a moment. "That he's dead, yes. As to how he died—whether by accident, which I must admit would seem to be the case—I'm not quite so sure."

"Murder?" He looked at her steadily. "Why would anyone want to kill Rapley?"

"It hasn't occurred to you that in the dark someone could've mistaken him for you? Especially in that long black mackintosh which, I noticed, is identical to the one you were wearing and to Inch's."

"I—" He hesitated, his brow gathered in a deep frown. "No . . . frankly, the idea never crossed my mind." He paused, considered the suggestion. Then, shaking his head: "No, I don't really think so. No one would expect me to go out looking for Bruno. That's Inch's job."

"Is Inch in the habit of arming himself, as Rapley did tonight, with a shotgun when he goes out to fetch in the dog?"

Again he frowned. "I take your point. No. Neither would Rapley. Not normally. In fact never to my knowledge. Neither Inch nor Rapley had my permission to touch any of the firearms in the gun cupboard, though both knew, of course, where the keys of the cupboard are kept."

"Therefore Rapley took that gun along with him for some special reason."

He nodded slowly. "He must've spotted someone lurking about in the grounds—like he did earlier when O. P. was wandering about. And whoever it was out there must've seen the shotgun, known that Inch and Rapley weren't permitted to touch the guns, and mistook him for me." He paused, frowned. "But then, in that case there must've been some sort of struggle between Rapley and his assailant, which brings us back full circle. The shotgun still might've gone off accidentally. And once again, like an incident which occurred here last Thursday night, the sole purpose of the exercise might've been to frighten me."

"Killing Rapley, though, would surely achieve the same result. Only more forcefully so, wouldn't you agree?"

"Yes, I suppose so. . . . If they thought I wasn't taking them seriously enough." He hesitated and his eyebrows went up. "My sister-in-law told you about the stranger who called here and fired off several rounds of blank shots at me?"

She nodded. "And Rapley told me what happened at the theatre on Wednesday night after you were given the threatening note."

He looked surprised.

"May I see the note?" she asked.

From his wallet he removed a folded sheet of notepaper which he handed to her without comment.

The message, which was handwritten in a stubby black pencil, read, "You'll never get away with it, Flower!" and was signed, "The Bogeyman."

"The Bogeyman?" she inquired, looking up at him.

"My wife often left me little notes like that when she was going out and she knew I'd get in before her, and that was how she always signed herself. It was just one of those silly childish things young newly-weds often do," he explained with a small shrug.

"And the message? What significance did you place on it?"

"Well . . ." He paused, frowned a little. "The show, of course—*Abracadabra* . . . The way Jo is portrayed." He paused again, and then, as if anticipating her next question, he said, "I took a certain amount of literary licence with her character and personality. And why shouldn't I?" He spoke irritably. "She was the one who walked out, not me. She's asked for all she's got. And she needn't think she's going to get a penny out of me."

"Wouldn't you think she already knows that?"

He looked puzzled. The clairvoyante went on:

"Why else would she bother to go to all the trouble of trying to scare you the way she has?"

He nodded slowly. "Yes, I think I see what you're driving at. . . ."

"The photograph in your study—is that Jo?"

He smiled faintly. "Beautiful, isn't she? I should've known I'd never be able to hold on to her." He was silent for a moment, reflective. "It was a mistake, really—our getting married. She only wanted a good time, and I—well, I wanted a home and a family. Oddly enough, we never discussed this before we married. In fact I doubt that either one of us had given a second's thought to it— the question of having a family. It wasn't until afterwards—until, I guess, I started to see that these things were not for Jo—that I realized that this was really why I'd got married."

"But you never divorced her and found someone else who shared the same ideals as yourself?"

"No." He shook his head. "Male pride, I suppose. I can see now how stupid it was, but I was cocky enough to think she'd come back to me one day and settle down. And"—he sighed—"I was busy, the years drifted by. . . ." His voice tailed off wistfully.

"How successful were you when she left you?"

He smiled crookedly. "I didn't even have a foot on the bottom rung of the ladder. I didn't really start to go places until I sat down and thought about what you'd said to me after I'd asked you what you thought my chances were of making it to the top. I remember you laughed—which hurt a bit, I don't mind telling you—and then you said that you were hardly the right person to ask and that the answer lay within myself anyway." He smiled again. "At least I think you were the one responsible for that little pearl of wisdom. I can't remember now. . . . Anyway, I put the two pieces of advice together and came up with Gould and Skellern, the advertising agency Faye worked for. I'd heard they were good, the best, so I scraped together every penny that I could and then presented myself at their offices one day and announced that I had a brand new whiz-bang product which I was considering commissioning them to package and market for me." He laughed a little. "I can still remember the looks on their faces when I eventually got round to telling them that I was the product. By which time, I might add, they were in so deep they couldn't back out of handling me. Not without making complete fools of themselves. The rest is a matter of recorded history."

She folded up the sheet of notepaper, gazed at it for a moment, then handed it back to him.

He raised his eyebrows. "No comment?"

"About the note? Only that it might not have been written quite so recently as a week ago. If you look along the folds of the paper you'll see there's a faint ridge of accumulated dirt and grime."

He examined the creases carefully. "Yes, I see what you mean. Only I shouldn't place too much store by that, you know." He smiled up at her. "If you'd seen the grimy article who delivered it, you'd marvel that it's as clean as it is. I doubt that his body has touched the inside of a bathtub this side of last Christmas. His hands and finger-nails were filthy, covered in grease. I can't say for sure, but my impression was that he'd travelled by motor bike. He was dressed for it, anyway. All black leather and vicious metal studs sticking out all over him. Even on the leather dog-collar round his neck. You've never seen anything like it," he finished, shaking his head.

"Was the note in an envelope?"

"No, just like this. The lad who delivered it took it straight out of his jacket pocket." He was momentarily silent. Then he went on: "I always wanted a son, but when I see kids like that, I'm not a bit sorry that I never had any family. It would've only ended up in bloodshed. Theirs! I couldn't put up with it. I'd kill him—any son of mine who went round looking like that!"

Mrs. Charles smiled faintly. "When was the last time you saw your wife?"

He sighed. "A lifetime ago. That's how long it seems now. So much has happened since. . . ." His eyes became distant, and he spoke slowly. "Sometimes I even wonder if she's not some fantasy figure I've created in my mind. But no . . ." He brought himself up sharply with a frown. "Jo happened all right. Fifteen years ago," he said abruptly. "Something like that. I can't remember exactly." He shrugged. "Those years—I was working all over the place, a couple of nights in a club here, a week somewhere else— are pretty much of a blur to me now. Freda—my sister-in-law— would've had a better idea. Jo went to her for money after she left me," he explained. Then, after a slight pause: "I didn't know anything about this for quite a few years, not until Freda called to tell me that their—hers and Jo's—parents had died. Freda hadn't been able to trace Jo at the London address Jo had given her the last time they'd met—which I understand was in the buffet of the railway station in their home town—and Freda contacted me hoping that I'd be able to tell her where she could find her."

"Is this how Miss Cobb came to live with you?"

"Yes. She'd never worked—hardly ever set foot outside her parents' home, was never allowed to. Mr. and Mrs. Cobb had always insisted that she, as the oldest daughter, should stay at home and take care of them, and then when they died, she was left virtually destitute. Besides . . ." He paused, shrugged. "Well, I felt I owed her something. Jo and I had done nothing to further her cause. All we'd done was to make life twice as tough for her. The old people never knew anything about it until it was too late, but Jo used to climb out the bedroom window at night and go down to a local night-spot—a working men's club, actually—and serve behind the bar. That was where we met. I remember"—he smiled ruefully—"that one of the first things she said to me was that she didn't think I had much talent. The last night she climbed out of the bedroom window, it was to run off with me and get married. Unfortunately, poor Freda was left holding the proverbial baby, as it were, and the old people made her pay for it." He hesitated, frowned. "I suppose you noticed that she was—well, a little odd?"

"I did rather wonder about that business with Mrs. Gould up in Miss Cobb's bedroom," Mrs. Charles confessed.

"Yes . . ." He nodded. "That was bizarre, to say the least." He considered for a moment. "I think I suspected that something of the sort might've happened—that Freda might've gone to see Faye behind my back and given her the wrong idea about us, and that this was why Faye suddenly took off and married Maurice, a co-director. But I was never sure. And anyway, there was nothing I could do about it by then. I had too much respect for Maurice to make any attempt to come between Faye and him once they'd married, although at the time I was completely shattered by it."

Mrs. Charles nodded. Then she said, "I hope you won't take this as an impertinence, but your sister-in-law gave me to understand that you are suffering from a heart condition. She also led me to believe that this isn't common knowledge, none of your friends know anything about it."

He shrugged. "It's nothing too serious. Quite the usual sort of thing for a man of my age and build who works as hard as I do. I've just had one or two minor warnings that it's time I slowed down a little and lost some weight. Freda was always inclined to be a bit of an alarmist about everything."

"But you did collapse—both at the theatre when you received the note written by your wife, and here at your home when some-one fired blank shots at you."

"Wouldn't you?"

"On the second occasion, not the first."

He looked annoyed. "I hadn't heard a word—not one single word!—from my wife since the night she cleared out on me. . . . For all I knew she could've been dead! I was knocked sideways, literally bowled over when I opened that note and realized who it was from. It was the unexpectedness of it. . . . Years of absolute silence and then *that!*"

"Why do you suppose your wife did things this way instead of having, say, a direct confrontation with you about the show, or instructing a lawyer to sue you for defamation of character?"

He looked at her steadily. "If I knew the answer to that one, my wife would still be with me. I'd have understood her better, what her needs were, and would never have lost her the way I did."

"Was there another man involved?"

"Not as far as I know. I doubt it. Freda didn't think so either. At least this was the impression Jo gave her during the half-hour or so they sat drinking tea together in the station buffet. It was a simple straightforward hankering for the bright lights of the big city and non-stop fun—a wish to be free, single, again."

There was a long silence. Then Danny Midas asked, "Is there anything else?"

"Perhaps just one more question . . . Another impertinent one, I'm afraid," she warned him with a smile. "Who would stand to gain most by your death? Financially, I mean."

"Only my sister-in-law," he replied without hesitation. "Apart from a few minor legacies and bequests, everything went to her."

Mrs. Charles thought for a moment, then nodded. "Yes," she said slowly. "I daresay that makes sense. . . . That could be why your wife has gone about things the way she has."

He looked at her questioningly.

"Let us suppose that the shock of being fired at with blank shots had killed you on Thursday night and that your sister-in-law, Miss Cobb, had survived you," said the clairvoyante. "I have no doubt that in these circumstances, your wife could've made a successful claim against your estate for a share of it."

His expression hardened. "There's a clause in my will which states specifically that my wife is to receive nothing. I have also given my reasons for excluding her from my will."

"Maybe so. But even the most carefully of prepared wills can sometimes be overturned by the courts. A clever lawyer, a sympathetically presented case . . . It's happened."

"Not to my will, it won't," he said coldly. He rose to his feet. "Who shall I send in next? That is, if you've finished."

"Mr. Rosenberg, I think," she replied.

He looked at her hesitantly. "I realize that it could be a little early yet, but may I ask if you've reached any conclusions?"

"Only that I think you're right and there is a conspiracy and that it concerns your wife."

He frowned. "You will get to the bottom of it?"

"I wouldn't set my hopes too high if I were you."

He stared at her for a moment, then turned to leave.

"Oh," she said softly. "There was just one other thing. What was the colour of your wife's hair?"

"Whatever was currently in fashion!" he snapped back over his shoulder at her. "Red—auburn the last time I saw her. Blonde when we first met."

Frowning, he opened the door and went out.

She hadn't asked if the handwriting was Jo's and that puzzled him. He was quite certain the question hadn't been overlooked by her. She was a lot shrewder than he would've given her credit for. . . .

He paused thoughtfully in the hall. Freda . . . Yes, that was it. Freda told her it was Jo's handwriting. But all the same he was surprised that it hadn't been confirmed with him. After all, Freda was mad. Anybody with half an eye could see that. . . . Which was probably what that business concerning the will was all about. If Jo could've proved that Freda was mad—and she wouldn't have had much difficulty with that one!—Jo could well have inherited everything.

Satisfied with this reasoning, he continued on out to the kitchen calling Bennie's name.

CHAPTER 16

Call the Next Witness!

O. P.—like the usher of a court—took up the call, altering the tone of his voice each time he called out Bennie's name so that it resembled an echo.

"Oh, for heaven's sake, O. P.," Cappy growled. "Grow up!"

Bennie rose nervously from the table around which everyone was sitting drinking freshly brewed tea and half-heartedly nibbling hot buttered toast. He started for the door.

"I'll come and call you in a few minutes and say your mother wants you," said O. P. mockingly.

Bennie shot him an anxious look and went out. By the time he reached the drawing-room he was perspiring heavily.

"Sit down, Mr. Rosenberg," said the clairvoyante pleasantly. "I've only a couple of questions for you which shouldn't take long."

He sat forward on the edge of the chair opposite her, gripping his knees tensely in his hands. "Yes?" he said cautiously.

"Mrs. Midas . . . Are you quite sure you've never met her?"

He nodded his head.

"But you nevertheless managed to discover quite a bit about her. At least this is the impression you gave earlier when you and Danny were talking, and you spoke of the private research you'd done on his life."

Bennie's mouth was cotton wool dry. With great difficulty, he gulped, "Yes," and confirmed it with a nod.

"If I promise that anything you say concerning Mrs. Midas goes no further than this room and our two selves, will you tell me what you discovered about her while you were doing this research?"

He frowned, thought for a moment. Then he said disgruntledly, "She wasn't common and cheap the way Danny insisted she should be painted. It's no sin to want a good time and be happy and free. Not every woman is cut out to be a wife and mother." He hesitated, gazed into the distance. "The way I see her, she was like some beautiful rare exotic bird that Danny wanted to keep locked up in a gilded cage—his prized possession—and when she got his drift, she simply waited her chance and then when he wasn't looking, she up and flew away. Just like she'd done to her parents when they'd tried the same thing with her." He looked abruptly at Mrs. Charles and said fiercely, "I hated what Danny made me do to her. It wasn't necessary. . . ."

"Then why did you do it?" she asked him quietly.

His eyes suddenly swam. "For the oldest reason in the world. Money. Against the advice of my mother, I made an unwise investment—backed a friend, a property developer, with everything I had, lost the lot. Including my mother. She had a stroke—the shock killed her. Nobody wanted to know—all my so-called friends deserted me—and I was sick and broke, ready to put up the copyrights of my other shows as collateral. . . . That was how desperate I was. And then along came Danny Midas with his proposition, and I took it, grabbed it with both hands."

He frowned earnestly at Mrs. Charles. "I'm not saying this to justify what I've done, but I was just about finished—all washed up. I don't think I'd ever have written another word or note of music if he hadn't come along when he did. Even after I'd signed with him, it was weeks before I could sit down and work at the piano. I'd completely dried up. The worry and despair over my mother and my financial situation had left me totally drained. And I don't care what anybody says, *Abracadabra* is not my best work—not by a long chalk! I know when I've written something good. There's not really all that much of Bennie Rosenberg—the old Bennie Rosenberg who used to write smash hit musicals—in it. It's the Danny Midas legend that carries it along, makes it what it is. Joe Bloggs, the plumber's mate, could've written the words and music, and it still would've been a big hit," he finished bitterly.

"No," said the clairvoyante with a small smile. "I don't think so."

"You're very kind, but I know when I've struck out," he said disconsolately.

"You only feel that way because Danny won't agree to the changes you want to make."

He leaned towards her, frowned. "You've seen the show. His

wife only appears briefly in the first act, and she was never part of the Danny Midas legend, anyway—she walked out on him years before he hit the big time. That segment could be cut out completely, and the only difference it would make would be to tighten and improve that first act, get it moving, which it doesn't do now. But will Danny hear of it?" His eyes widened angrily. "Two words I changed in the first act last Wednesday night, and he spotted them. . . . Those two coarse expletives Mrs. Midas uses in that row she has with Danny shortly before she clears off. They're quite out of character. Even the actress playing her part says she winces inwardly every time she has to use them."

Bennie's eyes grew even wider. "He's obsessed about her, you know. Absolutely obsessed! I'm seriously beginning to wonder if he's not deliberately trying to force her out into the open so that they can have some sort of showdown with one another. Let's face it, she got the better of him, and as near as I can tell, she's the only person who ever has. And it still rankles him. He'd dearly love to get even with her."

Mrs. Charles nodded thoughtfully. Bennie waited for her to say something, but when she remained silent, he leaned back and said tiredly, "There are only two people in my entire life that I have ever been truly afraid of. One was my father, who thought I was effeminate, unmanly, because I wanted to be a musician, and the other is Danny Midas. He—Danny—will destroy me, cut me down as surely as he's built me back up, if you break your word and tell him what I've told you. He's got very powerful connections in the theatre. He could see to it that I never work again. Even if I had the money to back my own shows, he'd make sure I'd never find a theatre to stage them in."

"I won't tell him," she promised. She hesitated. Then: "Those changes you made to the dialogue on Wednesday night—were you in the theatre for that particular performance?"

He nodded. "Danny was there too—with a woman. I didn't see them, but I went backstage during the show to talk to the cast, and Charlie—the doorman—told me that Danny and some woman had turned up at the stage door half-way through the first act. Danny was so worked up about the changes I'd made that he had some kind of fainting fit as he was making his way backstage and had to leave before talking to any of the cast or me. Of course, when I found out that he'd been there, I instructed the cast to go back to the original dialogue—there were a couple more changes in the last act which, in my opinion, is a bit like the first and needs tightening up. He'd only have taken it out on them—and her in particular, the young kid playing Mrs. Midas—and that wouldn't have been fair. She was only doing what she'd been told."

Mrs. Charles nodded her head. Then she said, "Thank you, you've been very helpful. Do you think you could ask Mr. Oliver to come in now, please?"

Bennie rose and went to the door. Hesitating, he turned and said, "I didn't cut those telephone wires. I know it looks bad, my saying I phoned my mother, but—" He paused, looked distressed. "Sometimes, when I get very upset, I really do think she's still alive, and it's not until I dial my home phone number, and it keeps on ringing and ringing and no one answers that I suddenly remember that she isn't there any more."

"You did actually try to get through to your home?"

"Yes, and the phone was ringing, so there was nothing wrong with the line then. It had to be sometime after I came back in here that somebody cut the wires."

He looked away, thought for a minute about what he had said, then nodded, opened the door, and disappeared.

CHAPTER 17

The Evidence of the Musical Director

O. P. slouched in the chair grinning at Mrs. Charles.

"I've read about how cute some of you clairvoyantes are at giving cold readings," he said. "That's what you call it, isn't it? When what you're really doing is guessing. . . . You make a statement—if it lands on fertile ground, the other person, the one you're doing the reading for, me, reacts favourably, you spot the reaction and then step by step build on it, telling me things about myself that I think you couldn't possibly know and yet I'm the silly so-and-so who's actually giving you all the information about myself." His grin widened, and he leaned forward conspiratorially. "But don't let it bother you; your secret's safe with me. I won't tell any of the others how the trick works. We're all phoneys, anyhow, aren't we? In one way or another . . . Pretending to be what we're not."

He raised his eyebrows at the clairvoyante's faint smile. "Oh, that is good," he said. "Very enigmatic. Full of secret promise. The customers must love it. I'm almost tempted to ask you to tell me my fortune."

"If by that you mean you'd be interested to know what the future holds for you—"

He held up a hand. "Hold everything right there. You've met my brother Denis, haven't you? The producer? You talk just like him." He waved his hand about. "But carry on . . . You were saying?"

"What I was going to say is that you've got very little future ahead of you."

"Rubbish," he said. "I'm really quite brilliant. Too good for that lot out there. I drink to deaden the agony of the truly mediocre company I'm forced to keep. And that includes Danny Midas, one of whose fans I'm not, never was, and never will be."

"Forced?"

"Well, it's my lovely brother, isn't it? The one who talks like you. Or maybe it's the other way round; you talk like him." His hand floated about again. "Whichever way it is. He thinks I'm letting down the side and all that. The family . . . Y'know, all the people who make sacrifices to give me the kind of things he wanted and never got." He frowned suddenly. "I'm not boring you, I hope, dear lady."

"Not at all," she said. "However, I wasn't actually referring to your professional future. Not specifically."

"Oh dear," he said. "Do I detect ominous overtones to that remark? Ah, yes . . ." He nodded. "I get it. The cold reading . . . You've observed how much I drink—as a matter of fact, I do myself an injustice there, I'm really an alcoholic. . . . Well, almost," he added, grinning, "and you're going to predict a sad, untimely end for me."

"True," she admitted. "But not for that reason. The untimely end you're going to meet will be brought about—if you'll forgive me for saying so—because you really do think you're too good for 'that lot out there,' as you put it. An erroneous belief, Mr. Oliver, that could cost you your life."

He looked at her. The room went very quiet. Then Mrs. Charles said smoothly, "And that, Mr. Oliver, is a classic example of a cold reading. . . . The kind done by Hercule Poirot of the little grey cells, I might add, and not Madame La Zonga! You're treading a dangerous path. Be warned."

O. P. hesitated. Then, with a grin, he said, "*Garn* . . . You're guessing! My face never gave a thing away."

"No, but your shoes did." The clairvoyante smiled at the startled look on his face. "When we all gathered in the hall soon after hearing the shot which killed Rapley, your shoes—like Inch's, who we all know went outside—were wet, muddy-looking. You were outside when Rapley was shot. And I think you either shot him, or you saw who did."

O. P. stared at her. Then, with a slow smile, he said, "You're at it again, aren't you? Guessing?"

She shook her head.

No one spoke. O. P.'s smile faded. Then he said, "All right, so I was outside. But it still doesn't make any difference. I don't know any more than the rest of you do. I heard the shot, yes, but I didn't see anything. Or anyone. As a matter of fact, I thought the shot came from in here. I was round the back in the garage checking the car engines." His eyebrows went up. "The rotor arms really are missing, you know."

"Did you really think they would be there?"

"I wouldn't have trusted Rapley any further than I could've thrown him."

"A sentiment, I would suspect, that someone else shares with you."

He looked at her for a very long moment. Then he said slowly, "You think he was murdered, don't you?" His brow furrowed. "Why would anyone want to kill him?"

"The most logical explanation for his death would seem to be that it was a case of mistaken identity. Somebody mistook him for Danny Midas."

O. P. whistled softly. "So our beloved employer isn't quite so mad after all. Somebody really is out to get him. And not me, dear lady. I know next to nothing about guns. Can't bear the nasty noisy things," he added in a fair imitation of the way Bruce spoke.

"Did you give Mrs. Gould Bruce's gun?"

O. P. narrowed his eyes. "I cannot tell a lie. . . . I most certainly *didn't!* I'm a bit past those childish sort of games. And so was Faye. Though I don't doubt that whoever stole his gun from him gave it to her to give back to him. It's what I would've done; that's if I had half-inched it from him, which, as I've said, I didn't. Faye and Bruce got on well together. He could always run and cry on her shoulder and be assured of a sympathetic audience, which is more than can be said for the rest of us. With the exception of Lilla, of course. Lilla's everybody's pal. She's the only one out of the lot of us who plays it really straight, y'know. Don't trust any of the rest of us. We're much too wrapped up in ourselves and our own individual ulterior motives for anything we might say to be worth anything. Even I don't believe half of what I say"—he grinned— "and I certainly don't believe a word of anything *they*"—he inclined his head at the hall—"might tell me. With Danny Midas heading the list of people I least trust. That man is a snake. I still can't figure out why the likes of my brother and Teddy Cummings worship the ground he slithers along, and break out in a cold sweat at the thought of something happening to upset their peachy little world."

The clairvoyante considered him thoughtfully. "Would I be right in thinking that Ray Newman could feature in these fears of Mr. Cummings'?"

He laughed. "You don't miss much!" He shrugged. "Ray's going to replace Teddy for next season's TV series."

"Your brother told you that?"

"Not in so many words. Ray wasn't named specifically. But there's definitely going to be a replacement, and as a casual, totally disinterested observer, I'd say that that person is going to be Ray. That's where this punter is going to put his money, anyway."

"Not if Lilla—Miss Osborne—is right about the way Danny hires new people. According to her, the winner in this sort of situation is always a rank outsider. Ray Newman, you might say, is the hot favourite."

He thought for a moment. Then, grinning, he said, "I like it! Can't think why I didn't see it. That's exactly what'll happen. And now that you mention it, I seem to remember my brother telling me once that this was more or less how Teddy got the job in the first place—as the rank outsider nobody gave a second glance. Funny how these things come full circle. . . ."

O. P. spent another five minutes with the clairvoyante discussing the various methods Danny Midas employed to dismiss staff, and then he went out with instructions to request Ray Newman to come in next.

CHAPTER 18

The Evidence of the Losers

The interviews with both Ray Newman and Teddy Cummings, who followed him, were very similar. In strict confidence, Ray Newman confessed that he was to replace Teddy for next season's TV series (and therefore had everything to lose if anything happened to Danny Midas meanwhile—a point he stressed several times). And in even stricter confidence, Teddy Cummings admitted his fears that he was about to be replaced by Ray. Which possibly gave him a motive for killing Danny Midas . . . Though surely not before he knew for certain whether the cold winds of change really were going to blow unfavourably in his direction, the clairvoyante thought to herself as Teddy got up to leave.

Danny Midas was to be congratulated on his handling of the situation. Neither man seemed remotely aware of the possibility that there might be a third contender to keep a watchful eye on, which convinced the clairvoyante that Lilla was right, there was someone else in line for the job. The clairvoyante also thought she knew who that person might be, and again it was Lilla who had given her a clue. . . . A peculiar, knowing little smile that always seemed to be on her lips now whenever she looked at Leo Polomka.

CHAPTER 19

The Evidence of the Winner

Leo did not deny it. He was to replace Teddy. The contract had already been drawn up. . . . Signed, sealed, and delivered, he admitted to the clairvoyante.

He smiled a little at the thoughtful expression on her face. "You are surprised, yes? at a theatrical set designer getting the plum job of magical adviser to Danny Midas."

"No, not really. Not when I know that you and Miss Osborne were once married to one another."

"Ah, she told you about that. Her father . . ." Leo nodded his head. "A brilliant man—a little old-fashioned, but, yes, I learnt a lot from him. Unfortunately, it has taken me all these years to find the right outlet for my own magical talents. Meanwhile I have had to content myself with the next best thing, as far as I was concerned. My stage sets—well, you've seen them for yourself and remarked upon them—they really are quite outstanding. Uniquely different. In so many ways like a magic trick, a good illusion, where I, the designer—like the magician with his magic wand—create a belief in the reality of something that is not really there."

He smiled patronizingly at Mrs. Charles. "So you see, madam, this for me is the chance of a lifetime to do the thing I have always wanted to do, dreamed of doing. The next series of *The Midas Touch* will be the best ever. You must not miss it. Why then should I wish to kill Danny? Not for money! I would do this series for him gladly, willingly, for nothing. I do not even know Mrs. Midas, I have never met her. Nor do I have any wish to meet her. Not if she is the kind of person who thinks so little of bringing such misery to those who love her."

"Danny Midas, you mean?"

He nodded. "Oh yes . . . You must pay no attention to the show. That is only make-believe. Danny doesn't hate her. He's never hated her. He loves her. He will never love anyone as much as he loves her. She was a very foolish girl to be so impatient. She should've had more faith. Look at me!" he said with an expansive smile. "All the years it has taken me to get what I want. But I got it in the end, didn't I? Oh, I know Danny's act in those days, when he and Jo were first married, was pretty terrible. But the talent, the star quality, was there. Everybody said so. Except Jo, of course. She was so sure he'd never make it." He shook his head solemnly. "Yes, she should've been patient, had just a little more faith. . . ."

"You saw Danny's early act?"

He nodded, grimaced politely, almost apologetically. "It was the gold lamé suit—that was his real mistake. He got caught up in this idea of 'The Midas Touch'—his catch-phrase—and got carried away with it. No, the suit was all wrong. Very immature. Corny. Once he'd got rid of that—and all his other strange notions about how he should look, this fixation with an all-gold appearance—his talent got through, and he was on his way. A good wife should've been able to advise him there. But as it was"—he sighed—"that was something left to Faye—Mrs. Gould—to do. She made Danny Midas what he is today. She was so very much in love with him. It was very sad. They should've married. But then, that would've been a fairy story ending, and life's not like that, is it? Life is very often loving and wanting someone you can't have, or you think you can't have, and then shooting yourself when you realize that you might've made a terrible mistake." He frowned. "I'm referring, of course, to that strange business tonight upstairs in Miss Cobb's bedroom." He was quiet for a moment. Then: "It was so unlike Faye. . . . To behave like that in front of everyone. And to have such a silly notion about that poor woman and Danny."

"You don't think there's anything in it?"

"That Miss Cobb was Danny's wife?" He hesitated. Then he said, "I'll put it this way: she wasn't Jo Midas."

"But you said you've never met her."

"No, that is quite true, I haven't." He spoke hesitantly, frowned. "But I caught a glimpse of her once at a night-club. Someone—the person I was with that night who knew Danny and Jo—pointed her out to me and told me that she was Danny's wife. This would've been about two or three months before she and Danny split up. She's the girl in the photograph in the study, only much much more beautiful in real life. But"—he shrugged—"who knows? Maybe Danny divorced her."

"And then married the woman upstairs?"

He shrugged again. "If he says she's his sister-in-law, then that's good enough for me. Danny wouldn't lie about something like that."

"There are some people who might take you up on that point."

"Then it is those people, whoever they may be, whose motives I would question, madam, not Danny's."

Leo got to his feet, hesitated. "I wonder if I might be permitted to ask you a question? It's about the door of the toilet in the cloakroom. I heard what Danny and Ray said—that there is a bullet hole in it—but I felt that there was something else, something you'd noticed and were keeping to yourself. You can trust me, you know. I'm the one person you can trust. Danny will tell you that."

"I only saw what Danny and Mr. Newman could see," she replied. "There was nothing else."

He looked at her thoughtfully. Then, after a moment, he nodded. "Yes, perhaps I was letting my imagination run away with me a little there. But still, it was a very strange thing. . . ." he said slowly. "That bullet hole in the door."

"I found Miss Hirsch's explanation perfectly logical in the circumstances."

He thought for a minute, then nodded again. "Who shall I send in next?" he asked.

"Mr. Neville, if you wouldn't mind," she replied.

She watched him go out. Did he know she didn't trust him, or was he so sure of himself that his assurance was little more than mere formality? He might not be involved in a plot against Danny Midas—in fact, she knew he wasn't—but he was nevertheless one person she would now never take into her confidence. And that, to date, made a total of four—the three people whom she believed to be involved in a conspiracy and Leo Polomka whose own personal self-interest in the continuing well-being of Danny Midas made him perhaps the most dangerous and untrustworthy of all.

CHAPTER 20

The Accused

Bruce came in, thin-lipped, hostile. He sat down tensely on the extreme edge of the chair.

"I object most strongly to this," he began. "What right have you got to interrogate people? Anything I've got to say I'll say to the police, the proper authorities. And I'm not going to talk to them, either, without my lawyer present."

"What is happening out in the kitchen at the moment?" inquired Mrs. Charles.

He blinked at her. "What? Oh . . ." He frowned. "Nothing much. Bennie's gone upstairs to lie down. He said he was feeling squeamish. The others . . ." He shrugged. "They're just sort of sitting there, not saying anything, just waiting their turn to be sent for."

"Well, at least they've stopped accusing you and Mr. Inch of things you haven't done."

He stared at her. Then his eyes narrowed suspiciously. "You don't expect me to fall for that one? You're just like them. You think we killed Rapley. Well, I'll say this just one more time—and this is all you're going to get out of me—Mr. Inch and I had nothing to do with what happened to him. It was an accident, like Danny said."

She nodded. "Fair enough. There were really only two questions I wanted to ask you, anyway, Mr. Neville, and it's entirely up to you whether you answer them or not. One concerns Mr. Rapley— a comment he made earlier this evening when reporting back to Danny that somebody had been tampering with the cars—and the other is about your gun."

"What about my gun?" he asked cautiously.

"When did you lose it?"

"I didn't lose it. Somebody stole it—either during the party Danny threw after the show on opening night, or afterwards while I was getting O. P. home. It was in my shoulder-bag, which was lying on the back seat of my car with some papers. I started out with O. P. sitting in the front with me, but he made such a nuisance of himself—he'd had a real skinful, I can tell you!—that I had to stop the car and get him out and into the back. That was when I reckon he must've stolen my gun from my bag—while he was lying on the back seat."

"The gun was definitely in your bag when you left the party?"

"I . . ." Bruce hesitated. "Well, yes, I think so."

"You don't know for sure?"

"Well, no . . ." Bruce looked flustered. "I didn't actually look in my bag and check that it was there. I had no need to—to go to my bag for anything, I mean. I keep all my keys, including the ones for the car, on a small chain which is clipped to the belt on my trousers."

"So in other words, somebody could've stolen the gun during the party. Was your bag with you all the time?"

Again he hesitated. "No . . . Some of the time it was in the administrative office." He frowned. "I suppose somebody could've stolen it then. . . . The office isn't kept locked or anything, and people were coming and going—wandering about all over the place—all the time." He paused, and his frown deepened. "Come to think of it, O. P. was in there for a while on his own—flaked out on the couch. And it's just the sort of thing he would do," he said petulantly.

"Maybe somebody else thought that too."

"You mean"—his eyes widened—"somebody else stole my gun and knew I'd blame O. P. for it?"

"Would Faye do something like that?"

Bruce looked most indignant. "She was my friend. She'd know how upset it would make me." His eyes suddenly filled with tears. "That gun has great sentimental value to me. It used to belong to a very dear friend of mine—my partner, Bobby. We had an animal act with two tigresses, and he used to wear the gun on stage as part of his costume. Only for effect, of course. He never had to use it. Bella and Ginny wouldn't have harmed a hair of Bobby's head."

As he finished speaking, Bruce burst into tears. He got out his

handkerchief and wept noisily into it for a few moments, then he
dried his eyes, put away the handkerchief, and then, as if nothing
had happened, he sniffed loudly and said, "You wanted to ask me
something about Rapley?"

Mrs. Charles nodded. "He made some reference to a conversation he'd had with Danny, which he seemed to think Miss Hirsch
might've overheard and misconstrued."

Bruce nodded quickly. "Rapley is jolly lucky Danny didn't fire
him on the spot. Twice it'd happened. Danny sent somebody to
the café round the corner from the theatre to fetch Rapley, and
both times he wasn't there. He wasn't far away, as it happened, on
either occasion—only upstairs in the flat over the café chatting up
the café owner's daughter. But he shouldn't have done it. Not
when he was on duty and when he'd already been hauled over the
coals once for doing it. I've never seen Danny so angry about
something—especially the second time when it was really important to him that Rapley was where he was supposed to be when he
was needed urgently. Someone at the theatre told me that Danny
was suddenly taken ill—during the show, I think, I'm not really
sure—and Miss Cobb, who was with him at the time, had to go and
fetch Rapley who, as I've said, wasn't where he was supposed to
be. Miss Cobb was terribly upset about it, and that probably put
the lid on it as far as Danny was concerned—her having to rush
about like a mad thing trying to find Rapley and getting all upset
and unnecessary when she wasn't really a hundred per cent fit
herself."

"Was Danny going to fire Rapley?"

Bruce shrugged. "I would've said so. . . . Eventually. He asked
me to draft out an advertisement for a new chauffeur. But then
again, that was in the heat of the moment."

"Was Rapley aware of this?"

"Possibly. I don't really know. I certainly didn't say anything to
him about it."

"Did you mention the matter to Mr. Inch?"

Bruce looked deeply hurt. "No, I most certainly did not! It
would only have upset him. And anyway, Danny wouldn't have
done anything about Rapley—dismissing him—until he'd got a
suitable replacement all lined up. That's not the way Danny does
things. And it's not that easy to get staff nowadays. It might've
taken months to replace Rapley."

"Yes," said Mrs. Charles meditatively. "I seem to remember your saying that Danny has a fairly high turnover in domestic staff."

Bruce nodded. "More so than average, I'd say. I don't really know why. . . . He's got rid of some really first-class people since I've been with him. I honestly think that at heart he's a misanthrope. He gets bored with people—the same faces—after a time and wants a change. I won't last much longer with him," he said matter-of-factly. "Neither will the Inches. They're doomed too."

"He sounds a very unhappy man," she observed.

"Frustrated," he said crisply. "He's really a failure, you know. A complete and utter failure! And she did that to him. His wife—Jo. You can't really claim to be a successful person if your private life doesn't match up to your professional one. And his private life is a wash-out, a mess! He should've divorced his wife, found himself someone else—and I thought he had in Faye—married her, and had the son he's always wanted. He pretends he doesn't care any more and that he wouldn't take her, his wife, back at any price, but he's always secretly hoped that one day she'd come back to him."

Bruce's eyes misted over. "For some people there's only ever one person, and if something happens to that person—they go away or die—nobody can ever really take their place."

Mrs. Charles nodded sympathetically. Then, after a suitable pause, she said, "Do you think you could ask Mr. Inch to come in now?"

He looked mildly alarmed. "You won't say anything to upset him will you? He's had a very nasty shock. And he's extremely distressed that Mrs. Inch thinks so badly of him."

Mrs. Charles gave him the assurance he sought, and he got up and went out. It was almost seven o'clock. Another hour and a half, and the coach should be there. The clairvoyante hoped that it would be on time.

Rising from her chair, she went first to the windows and then to the French doors and opened the curtains to a clear sky and pale yellow sunshine. It was going to be a lovely day. For some, she thought, turning with a smile as Inch knocked softly and came in with a tray of tea and toast for her.

CHAPTER 21

Inch by Inch

The butler put down the tray and then went round switching off the various table lamps scattered about the room. When he had finished, he looked inquiringly at Mrs. Charles, who indicated to him to be seated. He hesitated momentarily before complying, almost as if he did not consider this a proper thing for him to do.

"Thank you for the breakfast," she said, smiling. "I hadn't realized how hungry I was until I smelt the toast."

"It's been a very long night, madam," he said. His tone was remote, aloof.

"Is there anything you'd particularly like to tell me?" she asked, not looking at him and starting on the toast.

"No, madam. I don't think so. The police will be here shortly. I think it best if I talk to them."

"I quite understand," she said, nodding. "But perhaps you should wait a few more minutes before returning to the kitchen. The others might think it's a little strange if you don't spend some time with me."

He frowned a little, then nodded.

"Have Miss Osborne and Mr. Rosenberg come down?" she inquired conversationally. "Mr. Neville said Mr. Rosenberg was feeling unwell."

"They both came down a few minutes ago," replied Inch. "I think Mr. Rosenberg is feeling a little better now. Though he did say he felt rather depressed. Sickness and death have that effect on some people. They can't cope with it. It makes them moody, withdrawn—something of a hypochondriac."

"Would you say that this was how Miss Cobb's recent bout of ill health affected Mr. Midas?"

"Not perhaps in quite the same way that Mr. Rosenberg would appear to be reacting. But, yes, I would've said the fact that Miss Cobb was not well depressed Mr. Midas and maybe made him question his own mortality. Though this would've been before I knew that somebody was actually threatening to kill him. Now I'd be more inclined to think that his preoccupation with death and dying was linked more with this than with Miss Cobb's poor state of health."

"Did he ever discuss the possibility of his dying soon, either with you or Mrs. Inch?"

"No, madam." Inch shook his head. "But his lawyer called on Saturday afternoon, and while I was pouring drinks for them, I overheard Mr. Midas say that he wanted Mr. Sylvester—his lawyer —to draw up a codicil to his will. He said there were a number of additional charitable bequests he wished to make. At that point, madam, I left the room; I heard no more of their conversation. However, first thing next morning—that would be yesterday morning—Mr. Midas instructed Bruce and Rapley to bring down the wooden trunk—the chest containing all his old magic appara- tus—from the attic room and leave it in a more conspicuous place. He didn't say why, but having overheard some of his conversation with Mr. Sylvester the previous afternoon, my feeling was that he had convinced himself that he too was seriously ill and about to die, and he was afraid that his wishes with regard to the magic apparatus—it is to be buried at sea with his ashes—would be over- looked if the trunk were left with all the other old things he's got stored up in the attic."

Mrs. Charles nodded slowly. "He would certainly seem to have become suddenly preoccupied with the idea of his dying. . . . Though, as you've said, quite understandable in the circumstances —the threat made to his life coupled with the knowledge that his very sick sister-in-law might die at any moment from serious heart trouble."

"Quite," said Inch. "Miss Cobb had been giving him cause for concern for some months. Her doctor more or less warned him— and Mrs. Inch—that things could and probably would happen the way they did."

"What sort of relationship did Mr. Midas and Miss Cobb have with one another? How well did they get along?"

"On the surface, very well. However, it was my feeling that

deep down inside her, she was afraid of him, careful never to
overstep the mark, if you follow my meaning, madam. And I think
this was borne out by the things she used to say to Mrs. Inch about
him behind his back. . . . Things a real lady would never have
dreamt of saying to a member of the domestic staff. And all of it
quite without justification, I would hasten to add. Very possibly she
resented her dependence on him, and this was her only release for
her hostility towards him because of it. Miss Cobb was never, in my
opinion, truly at ease in the role she played as his housekeeper/
companion. I think it worried her greatly that she would in some
way 'show him up,' as it were. She used to sit some nights watching
him, never taking her eyes off him for one moment, almost as if she
wanted to ask him something but hadn't the courage. In some
ways she reminded me of a small child who has tried desperately
hard to please someone and is now waiting for a word of praise and
encouragement. . . . Although latterly, this habit of hers of
watching him all the time did tend to take on a rather more
sinister overtone. Mrs. Inch believes Miss Cobb was fully aware of
her condition even though, at Mr. Midas' request, the doctor
hadn't discussed it with her. And I think she felt cheated that Mr.
Midas was going to outlive her, and she deeply resented him for
it."

Mrs. Charles nodded pensively. "Mrs. Inch, you said, has had
some nursing experience. . . . Did she ever express any opinion
to you regarding Miss Cobb's mental state?"

He hesitated. Then he said, "Only once, madam. This was after
one of Miss Cobb's more bitter outbursts about Mr. Midas. Mrs.
Inch commented afterwards that she feared Miss Cobb was becoming unhinged, suffering delusions."

"Mad?"

"Slowly going that way."

"Did Mr. Midas ever discuss her mental state with Mrs. Inch?"

"No, never. He's not that kind of man. It was only Miss Cobb
who forgot her place. . . . Not that the poor woman could be
blamed for that if her mind really was going." Inch hesitated
again. Then, with a frown, he said, "Mrs. Inch thought it might've
been the divorce that finally turned Miss Cobb's brain. Miss Cobb
found out about it—that Mr. Midas' lawyer had had the notice
published in some obscure trade journal so that Mrs. Midas
wouldn't know he'd divorced her. . . . This, I would think, is

principally what upset Miss Cobb, though I'm not sure. I only know what she told Mrs. Inch—and I freely confess that much of what she said about Mr. Midas wasn't particularly reliable and needed to be taken with a good pinch of salt. However, according to her, it was the law—Mr. Midas had to go about things this way because he didn't know where Mrs. Midas could be located for papers to be served on her. In those circumstances—or so Miss Cobb gave Mrs. Inch to understand—a public notice must appear in a newspaper. And Mr. Sylvester—Mr. Midas' lawyer—craftily picked out this obscure periodical, knowing it was most unlikely that Mrs. Midas would ever see the notice. The idea, presumably, was that Mrs. Midas should be given no opportunity to contest the divorce petition or apply for alimony. I personally felt that Miss Cobb was making it all up. She was really quite concerned that he would one day marry again and that she would then find herself turned out of his house with nowhere to go. However, if Mr. Midas is right about his wife hiring somebody to kill him, it would make what Miss Cobb said about a divorce seem rather more feasible, wouldn't it? If Mrs. Midas found out what Mr. Midas had done to her behind her back and she determined to get even with him for it. Not that anyone could blame him for what he did. She walked out on him."

Inch paused, seemed concerned. Then: "I've never discussed this—the divorce—with anyone other than Mrs. Inch; not even with Bruce, Mr. Neville. And I told Mrs. Inch she wasn't to talk about it either. It's none of our business. And we don't really know, do we? that it wasn't all in Miss Cobb's imagination. You see," he said earnestly, "it could well be that she was only expressing a fear."

Mrs. Charles nodded. She stacked up the breakfast things on the tray, and Inch rose to take them away.

"I think there's only Miss Hirsch left for me to see," she said.

He went to the door, paused, then turned back to face her.

"I knew Rapley was dead," he confessed woodenly. "I was just coming back inside when you started down the stairs. You knew that, didn't you?"

"Yes," she said.

"Why didn't you tell Mr. Midas?"

She didn't answer.

He went on, "I'd gone outside to see what was keeping Rapley.

Mrs. Inch said he hadn't come back inside, and she was beginning to wonder what had become of him. I had just stepped out onto the terrace when the gun went off, and I knew immediately what it was. I ran towards the sound. . . . It seemed to have come from the direction of the wood, but you can't always be sure. The wind sometimes plays tricks at night with noises coming from there. Anyway, that was where I headed . . . towards the wood. And there he was. Rapley . . ."

"Did you see anyone else?"

"No . . ." He shook his head. "I was too shocked, stunned, to think about anything like that. I just looked at him, saw there was nothing anyone could do, and came on back inside. I did it all without consciously thinking about what I was doing, madam. It was not my deliberate intention to be deceitful. My brain simply went numb. And then . . . Well, you came down, and it seemed the simplest thing all round to pretend that I was as much in the dark as everyone else."

"Why do you suppose Rapley didn't mind going out and fetching Miss Cobb's dog? I am right in thinking that this is one of your duties?"

"Yes, that is correct, madam. I don't really know why he was so willing to do it last night. He didn't give a reason; he just insisted that he would do it."

"Did you find this odd?"

"Yes, madam. Very odd, to say the least. He and Bruno hated one another, and quite frankly, he had no hope at all of getting Bruno to come inside. Miss Cobb and I were the only ones Bruno would take any notice of, and even then only when he was in the mood to be obliging and do as he was told. At the time, though, I was inclined to think it might've been because Rapley knew I'd be engaged for some while in seeing to it that everyone was settled down comfortably in their rooms. Bruno's barking got on Rapley's nerves as much as everyone else's, and he would've therefore been as anxious as anyone to see the dog shut up indoors for the night. Bruno is really more suited to city life. The distractions of the countryside are making him chronically neurotic."

Inch spoke of the dog's nervous disposition with such earnest conviction that the clairvoyante found it hard not to smile. She moved quickly on.

"Had Rapley ever handled a shotgun before?" she inquired.

"Never to my knowledge, madam."

"So it would not be out of the question to suggest that he might've had an accident—tripped in the dark, and the gun went off, killing him," she said musingly.

"That was how it looked to me, madam. Except . . ." Inch paused for some moments, as if making up his mind about something. Then, in a slow, thoughtful voice, he continued:

"I can't be sure now, but I don't recall seeing the gun. Not the first time I looked at him."

She frowned at him. Then she said quietly, "You realize what you're saying, don't you?"

"Yes, I think so, madam. Rapley was murdered, and whoever shot him was still out there. The gun was put under Rapley's body to make it look like an accident after I'd come back to the house. That's if I'm right, and there wasn't a gun the first time I looked. We were all meant to think that Rapley had taken the gun along with him, whereas in actual fact he did no such thing, he was unarmed."

"He, Rapley, was mistaken for Mr. Midas?"

"I doubt it, madam. It is my honest opinion that Rapley deliberately went outside last night to meet someone who then turned round and equally deliberately shot him."

But why not simply slip outside and meet that person? Mrs. Charles asked herself. Why make a song and dance about fetching in the dog? Was it because he needed some plausible excuse for going out again at that hour of night—a good reason for leaving the house, one he knew not even his employer would challenge?

"Who holds the keys to the gun cupboard?" she asked.

"No one, madam. They are just left loose in the top drawer of the desk in Mr. Midas' study. Anybody could've taken them and used them to unlock the gun cupboard."

"Can you tell me exactly how many people know this about the keys, where they might be found?"

He hesitated, frowned. "Mr. Midas—and Miss Cobb, of course, she knew where the keys are kept—Mrs. Inch, myself . . . oh, and Mrs. Gilbert, I daresay, the woman who comes in from the village each weekday to clean . . ."

"And Bruce," said the clairvoyante when he paused.

"Yes, madam. But Bruce didn't kill Rapley, I'm sure he didn't.

He couldn't have. . . . You saw him. He was upstairs—in his night-clothes."

"Yes," she said. "But that isn't to say he didn't give someone else the keys. Or tell that person where they could be found."

Inch was slowly shaking his head. "No, madam," he said firmly. "Bruce wouldn't dream of doing anything like that. Mrs. Inch has put this idea in your head, hasn't she?—because of my friendship with Bruce and our plan to go into business together at some future date. I have told her time and time again that she has absolutely nothing to worry about. Bruce and I have no intention of going ahead with any of our plans until I've fulfilled my obligations to her. I intend to stick by my agreement with her until she's sixty—that'll be in three years' time—and ready to retire, and Bruce is perfectly happy about this. Bruce had no reason to kill Rapley. None at all. Rapley might have wished to see Bruce dead, but it was never the other way round, I assure you."

"Then what if whoever shot Rapley did so in error, thinking he, Rapley, was Mr. Midas?"

Inch stared at her.

She went on, "How long ago was it that Bruce's friend, Bobby, was killed?"

Inch looked down at the things on the tray, frowned. "Seven years ago next Wednesday, madam," he said quietly.

"Bruce blames Mr. Midas for Bobby's death, doesn't he?"

Inch took a moment or two to respond. Then he said dully, "Yes, madam." He looked up quickly. "But Bruce wouldn't do what you're thinking, I know he wouldn't! He gets very overwrought about things, and sometimes he says silly, childishly dramatic things—like wanting to kill Mr. Midas, and wishing he was dead—but they're only words, madam. There's no real intent behind them. Bruce is too soft-hearted, he couldn't kill anyone. Nor would he conspire with some other person to kill Mr. Midas, as you've suggested, and give that person the gun cupboard keys. Why, the worry of something like that would give him a nervous breakdown!"

"Yes," she said softly. "That was what I was thinking."

CHAPTER 22

The Red Herring's Evidence

Cappy looked tired and vaguely irritable. She was nevertheless still very beautiful. It was that rare, unexpected kind of flawless beauty, thought Mrs. Charles as she studied her, at which one could not help but stare in silent wonder.

Cappy returned the clairvoyante's gaze unwaveringly. She knew the effect she had on people, male and female, so she did not bother herself about what might be going through the older woman's head. She found the clairvoyante's own appearance reassuring. Just lately, and particularly when Lilla was having one of her off days, the thought of growing old and ugly had made Cappy feel physically ill, nauseated. But this woman, the one sitting staring at her, who was probably younger than Lilla but not by all that much, had lost neither her looks nor her figure. Her complexion wasn't bad either. Quite wrinkle-free . . . At least from where Cappy was sitting.

As if reading the young woman's thoughts, Mrs. Charles suddenly smiled. Then, after a moment, she said, "I was thinking that it seems such a waste—to be as beautiful as you are and yet to have chosen not to stand in the spotlight but to work behind the scenes."

Cappy made a dismissive gesture with her hand. "You sound just like my father. . . ."

"He wanted you to go on the stage?"

Cappy shrugged non-committally.

"One usually associates the female parent with that sort of aspiration."

"I can't say he ever pushed me—not in that way—but he was disappointed that I didn't follow in his footsteps."

"He was an actor?"

Cappy shrugged again. "You name it, he did it," she said abruptly.

The clairvoyante looked at her thoughtfully. "I can't help feeling that your face is somehow familiar."

Cappy scowled a little. "Well, I've never seen you before, I'm sure of that!"

"That wasn't quite what I meant. You remind me of someone, but for the moment I can't think who."

Cappy gave her an odd look. Then, with a frown, she said, "Lilla?" She ran her fingers quickly through her hair. "Because of this? Lilla's hair is almost the same colour. Though that's a wig she's wearing."

"No . . . I don't think so." Mrs. Charles smiled quickly. "Never mind. It'll come to me."

"People often say that to me—that they think they've seen me someplace before, or that I remind them of someone. It's because they're embarrassed, and that's their way of covering up."

Mrs. Charles looked at her questioningly.

"People always stare at me. And then they get embarrassed about it, and so they make out it's because I remind them of someone—"

Cappy broke off, suddenly became alert as a heavy, slow-moving vehicle came up the drive towards the house. "That must be the coach now," she said, getting up and going over to the French doors and then looking out. "It's early, thank God."

Mrs. Charles glanced at the time. It was just after eight-fifteen.

"I was sure it wouldn't turn up," said Cappy. "Danny's such a liar."

She turned and moved swiftly across the room towards the door which opened before she reached it as Danny Midas and the others came in. Inch had gone to request the coach driver to join them immediately in the drawing-room.

CHAPTER 23

Consider Your Verdict!

The coach driver said his name was Wells. He raised no objection when Danny Midas told him there had been a change of plans and that he (Wells) was to turn round and drive straight into town and bring back the police. (Murray, the driver of the minibus, had warned him that Midas was "cuckoo" and to expect almost anything; in fact it even crossed Wells's mind that Midas and his house guests were playing some weird kind of charade.)

It was Mrs. Inch who objected.

She suddenly appeared in the open doorway and said sharply, "No! I want Hawkes. You drive into the village—it's not far—and fetch Hawkes here. You'll find him outside the Red Cockerel at nine sharp."

Danny Midas frowned at Inch, who said, "P. C. Hawkes, sir. He stations himself in his panda car outside the public house in the village every Monday, Wednesday, and Friday between nine and nine-thirty A.M. so that anyone with a problem can have a word with him about it if they want. It's since they closed down the police station at Brockelhurst, sir. P. C. Hawkes spends most of his day moving from one village to the next—has his regular visiting times in all of them."

Cappy muttered something which nobody heard. She looked thoroughly fed up.

"The village then," Danny Midas amended, and gave the coach driver directions for getting there.

"Am I to tell the constable anything special, sir?" inquired Wells, still not sure if this were part of a game.

"No," replied Danny Midas with a glance at Mrs. Inch which defied her to disagree with him. "Just say there's been an accident

and that Danny Midas would like him to attend here—at his home
—as soon as possible."

"We don't want silly rumours and gossip spreading like wildfire
through the village," he explained once the driver had gone. "It's
better that the constable comes here and quietly appraises the
situation, then he can radio back to police headquarters for someone from there to come out."

Mrs. Inch made a small, disgruntled noise, but she didn't say
anything. She went over to the French doors and remained there
until the coach had disappeared from sight. Turning, she then
answered the question Bennie was about to ask.

"Hawkes should be here in a little over half an hour."

"Just enough time for Her Honour the Judge," said O. P., "to
give us her verdict." He smiled faintly at Mrs. Charles. "Well,
which of us is it to be, Your Worship? Who are you going to clap in
irons and deliver up into the brawny hands of the law?"

"Ah," she said with a little smile, "first I must retire and deliberate. That's the usual procedure, isn't it?"

O. P. smiled to himself. He said, "My mistake. Deliberate, by all
means, dear lady. We'll all go out and have another cup of tea
while we wait, won't we, chums?"

Mrs. Charles said, "No, you all stay here and *I'll* go out." She
smiled. "I think I'd like a walk in the grounds to stretch my legs
and clear my head."

"You won't forget that time is of the essence, will you?" said
O. P. "Half an hour, and the law'll be here. And I wouldn't want
anybody to steal your thunder. Oh, and don't leave the paths. . . .
We wouldn't want any more nasty accidents, would we?"

Mrs. Charles turned to the butler. "Perhaps you wouldn't mind
accompanying me, Mr. Inch?"

He looked surprised by her request but acquiesced with a faint
nod.

"Shall I fetch your coat, madam? It's in the kitchen, I think."

"No, that won't be necessary, thank you," she replied. "I don't
intend to stay outdoors long. Ten minutes, no more," she promised
Danny Midas, going with Inch to the door.

O. P. crossed to the French doors and waited for the
clairvoyante and Inch to appear. "Want to bet we don't see her
again inside thirty minutes?" He turned slightly as Danny Midas

moved up and stood beside him. "Wherever did you find her?" O. P. asked him.

"She's supposed to be good," said Danny Midas with a shrug.

"Yeah, but at what?" O. P. dryly rejoined.

One by one the others drifted over to them.

Mrs. Charles and Inch were walking slowly across the lawn.

"They're going down to the swimming-pool," said O. P. after a moment.

"No, the guest cottage," said Bruce with a tiny frown.

CHAPTER 24

More Evidence?

Mrs. Charles and Inch walked in silence, immersed in thought. As they approached the stone steps leading down into the hollow and the swimming-pool, Mrs. Charles paused and turned. Inch, who had fallen a little behind, similarly paused and turned. He followed her gaze which appeared to be focused on the anxious faces peering out at them through the French doors.

"That would be Miss Cobb's bedroom above the drawing-room," observed Mrs. Charles after a moment.

"Yes, madam," replied Inch.

She nodded, looked about her. "I suppose it would've been somewhere around here that Rapley stood watching Mr. Oliver. . . ."

"I would think so, madam," he agreed. "Rapley said he saw Mr. Oliver near the pool so he would've had to be standing somewhere hereabouts."

She nodded again. Then, looking thoughtfully back at the house, she said, "I would very much like to ask you to do something for me, Mr. Inch." She turned her head slightly and looked at him quizzically. "The reason I hesitate is because of this. . . ." From the pocket of her black velvet evening jacket she removed a woman's nylon stocking. She held up the stocking so that it hung from thigh to toe, then she handed it to him.

Puzzled, he took it from her and looked at it.

"I found it down the side of Miss Cobb's bedside table," she explained.

He nodded. "Yes . . . When you placed her shoe on it. I wasn't sure, but I thought you'd picked something up."

"Was Miss Cobb an untidy woman?" she asked.

"No, madam," he said, returning the stocking to her. "Quite the reverse."

She nodded. Then she said, "Shall we start back now?"

They fell into step. Then, after a thoughtful silence, Inch asked, "Why should one of Miss Cobb's stockings make you hesitate to ask me to do something for you?"

She narrowed her eyes a little. "I don't know very much about the mind of a murderer, Mr. Inch, but as a professional clairvoyante I do know a lot about people. Most of us—and I include myself—are creatures of habit, strict adherents to a prescribed order of behaviour in a recurring set of circumstances. Make a bad mistake once, and the chances are—oddly enough—that one won't learn by that mistake but will make it again and again. Not quite the same mistake, perhaps, but a variation nevertheless of the same old theme. In my case it has been disastrous marriages. . . . Three—four if I count the one that never was," she said in a soft, distant voice.

The butler nodded, looked both wise and sad. "Yes, madam. I understand what you mean. People can mean well, can't they? have the very best of intentions, but it always seems to go the same way for them, no matter how hard they try to break the old pattern or how determined they are that the same thing will never happen to them again."

"Fortunately, Mr. Inch," said the clairvoyante, "most of us harm nobody but ourselves, whereas the hardened criminal, for example—perhaps the strongest adherent of all to a ritualistic pattern of behaviour—harms others. . . . Whether he be an expert safecracker who steals all one's valuables, or is a mass murderer who brutally takes other people's lives. It is the pattern of behaviour of this latter person, the person who has committed murder more than once, which concerns me at the moment. . . ." she went on slowly. "The way in which he commits his particular type of crime."

They both paused. Mrs. Charles continued:

"I would think that the man who makes a habit of killing—like the thief who's in the habit of cracking safes—will go about his job much the same way every time. Wouldn't you agree that a person who's killed once using a woman's nylon stocking and got away with it, would be likely to use that same tried and tested method again?"

Inch frowned at the stocking which was still in Mrs. Charles's hand. He looked confused.

They walked on a little way, and then Mrs. Charles paused again. They were nearing the house; a few more yards and their conversation might possibly be overheard by the people in the drawing-room who were making no pretence of their interest in them. O. P. had at one point even opened the French doors as if to go outside, but Danny Midas had stopped him. Judging by the look on his face, O. P. was still quarrelling with him about it.

Mrs. Charles went on talking to Inch in a low voice, and when she looked back at the French doors again, only Lilla and Bruce remained.

CHAPTER 25

The Secret Kept from Everyone Else

O. P. slouched bad-temperedly in a chair. "What a swizz!" he said with a scowl. "What the hell was she doing with that nylon stocking? Trying to flog it to Inch? God, could you imagine that old queer got up in high heels and stockings?"

"I don't think it's necessary for that sort of talk," said Leo. "Not in front of Mrs. Inch."

"Ssh," said Cappy quickly. She had opened the door a little and was peeking through the slit at what was going on in the hall. "She's coming. . . ."

"So is the law," came Bruce's voice from across the other side of the room. He looked at Danny Midas. "There's a police car coming up the drive."

"Saved by the bell," said O. P. irritably.

"Was Inch with Mrs. Charles?" Danny Midas asked Cappy.

She shrugged. "He was going upstairs. I think she might've asked him to fetch her something from her room."

Bruce said, "I'll go out and have a word with the constable, if you like."

"No," said Danny Midas. "I'll do it."

"Be gentle with him," O. P. called after him. "Especially if he's only a tender young PC."

Danny Midas and Mrs. Charles came face to face at the door. He paused and looked searchingly at her, then turned aside without a word and went to attend to the police constable.

Inch paused for a moment in the passage, then opened the door of the guest-room and went in. He was carrying a hammer and a chisel. He had never broken a lock before, and he didn't feel too happy about doing it now, even though he knew he had little to lose. He and Mrs. Inch were finished at Abracadabra; they couldn't stay on after what had happened even if Midas insisted that they should. The situation among the three of them—Bruce, Mrs. Inch, and himself—would, Inch felt, be quite intolerable. They would be at each other's throats all the time. It had been bad enough before. . . .

He crossed to the window and opened the curtains, then turned back to the connecting door. He could see immediately what Mrs. Charles had meant when she had spoken of the lock being on the wrong side. No doubt the fault of Rapley and Bruce . . . They hadn't been too happy about having to fetch down the chest from the attic and had obviously dumped it down across the door any old how without realizing that the lock on the chest was on the far side.

Inch went up to the chest and looked at it. He hadn't been able to understand why Midas had wanted it brought in here, one of the guest-rooms, when really the proper place for it, taking into consideration its contents, was downstairs in the study. Though it was getting a mite cramped in there, he conceded with a grunt as he hauled the chest back from the door so that he could get at the lock.

He straightened up and stared at the padlock on the hasp. It wasn't a particularly strong-looking one. A couple of good whacks on the chisel with the hammer, he decided, should break it off.

He went back to the bedside table where he had left his lock-breaking implements while attending to the curtains and then returned with them to the chest.

Midas was not going to like this, he thought, hesitating before striking the first blow. But he need only worry about that, he reminded himself, if Mrs. Charles was wrong about the nylon stocking.

He stooped over, placed the chisel in what looked a likely spot, hesitated again, and then smashed down hard with the hammer.

The padlock fell with a clatter onto the bare polished floor-boards.

He paused, listened for the sound of running footsteps, but no one came to investigate.

Quickly, he undid the hasp and lifted the lid.

He looked down into the chest, let out a choked gasp, stepped back involuntarily.

Mrs. Charles had warned him to expect the worst but not even a detailed description of the contents of the chest could have prepared him for the shock of actually taking a look at what was in there.

It wasn't the nylon stocking tied tightly round the neck of the mummified female remains which he found shocking, horrifying.

It was the hair.

Masses of it.

All red.

Danny Midas returned to the drawing-room fifteen minutes later.

"He must've thought his special treats had all come at once . . . having three dead bodies served up to him on one plate," drawled O. P., eyeing Danny Midas curiously. "Where is P. C. Plod now?"

"I left him looking at Rapley," replied Danny Midas.

"Has he put in a call for someone else to come out?" asked Mrs. Inch.

"No, not yet. He told me he'd do it shortly."

O. P. laughed. "My God, even he's got you all summed up and is checking out your story first."

Danny Midas said coolly, "There was no story to tell. He's simply getting his facts straight before he radios in a report."

O. P.'s eyes narrowed. "You've told him about Faye and the one upstairs?"

"No. I thought it better to let that wait until other more senior police officers get here."

"How long will that be?" demanded Mrs. Inch.

"As long as it takes," replied Danny Midas curtly.

"I'm not satisfied," she said querulously.

"No, neither am I," said O. P. He looked at Mrs. Charles accusingly. "You—if you'll pardon me for saying so—have turned out to be a right damp squib!"

"Don't push it, O. P.," Danny Midas warned him testily. "I've just about had enough—"

O. P. sprang out of his chair. His face reddened explosively. "You've had enough? Well, if that doesn't take the biscuit! What about us? You've had us running around in circles and jumping through hoops all night long. I don't give a damn about you—

whether *you've* had enough. I've humoured you, played *your* game, now you must play mine. You'll be sorry if you don't! We've all been good little girls and boys at taking our turn at being 'it,' now it's *her* turn," he said, pointing at Mrs. Charles.

"For goodness' sake humour him," said Leo irritably. "We'll get no peace until you do."

Danny Midas made an impatient gesture, and O. P. looked at Mrs. Charles and said in a dry voice, "I think that means you're 'it'!" Then when Inch and P. C. Hawkes—whom Inch, on coming down from the guest-room, had found wandering helplessly about in the hall—suddenly appeared in the doorway, O. P. waved them into the room and said gaily, "Oh, good! Two more. Come on in and join the fun. We're having a lovely game here. It's Mrs. Charles's turn to be in the chair."

P. C. Hawkes, a much older man than everyone had expected, gave him an odd look, then turned to Danny Midas and said, "I've radioed through to headquarters, sir. There'll be someone out shortly." He got out his notebook. "I think perhaps I should take down one or two details—that's if you wouldn't mind, sir."

"No, you don't want to bother with that dreary old stuff," said O. P. with a breezy wave of his hand. "We're not going anywhere. Neither's Rapley. And we've got plenty more like him tucked away, haven't we, chums?" he added with a sly wink at the others. "Sit down and relax, officer, while the sibyl here gazes in the crystal ball and reveals all."

Hawkes stared at him blankly for several moments, then looked hesitantly at Danny Midas. He was anxious not to antagonize him needlessly. It was well-known that Danny Midas and the chief constable were chummy, and with this thought uppermost on his mind, Hawkes decided that it might be wise to clarify his position with the duty sergeant. Better safe than sorry . . .

"I think I should check back with headquarters first, sir," he said truthfully. "Let them know what's going on."

Danny Midas nodded, and then with a quick glance at O. P., Hawkes went out. Drunk as a lord, the constable concluded, putting away his notebook and heading for the front door. In fact, on reflection they were a rum-looking lot all round. He'd heard about these theatrical folk, the weird things they got up to, the wild parties they gave. . . . And he'd never much cared for Midas. The wife never missed his show on the telly, but there was too much of the clever chit-chat for his liking, not enough magic. . . .

CHAPTER 26

Only an Illusion

Mrs. Charles did as O. P. directed and took what he termed "the witness chair."

As she sat down, she looked at Inch, who returned her gaze steadily. O. P., watching them, frowned to himself. He recognized that something unseen had passed between them, and it irritated him. "All right," he said crossly. "Which of us did it?"

Inch looked round at him sharply, but the clairvoyante merely smiled and said, "Did what, Mr. Oliver?"

"Plotted to bump off our beloved employer, of course," said O. P. "Isn't that what this has all been about? Or did I fall asleep, and you started to play some other game without telling me anything about it?"

"Something like that," she admitted, and he stared at her.

"I was only joking, you know," he said.

"Yes, I realize that," she replied. "Unfortunately, I'm not. And the name of this new game is murder." She smiled faintly at the expression on O. P.'s face. "But don't let it concern you, Mr. Oliver, that nobody bothered to tell you we were playing something entirely different. That too—keeping everyone in the dark—was part of the game, the main rule of play."

O. P. gave his head a quick shake. "I don't get you. You're talking about Rapley, I take it?"

"Not specifically. But he was murdered."

Mrs. Inch let out a small cry. "I knew it! I knew there was something wrong. He never would've touched those guns, never in a million years."

"He might've," said the clairvoyante, "if instead of going out to fetch in the dog, as he insisted on doing, he went out to meet someone, someone whom he had reason to fear, or to think might try to kill him."

There was a deep silence. Then O. P. said, "Go on, we're listening. Who was Rapley going outside to meet? I suppose you do know—"

"Rapley's arrangement to meet his killer after the rest of us had gone upstairs to bed was made in this very room in the presence of all of us."

O. P. said, "I certainly don't remember hearing Rapley make arrangements with anyone to blow him away."

Cappy said, "All I can remember him saying was that he was going out to get the dog."

Bennie chipped in quickly, "And the cars—don't forget what he said about them."

Cappy frowned. "Oh yes, I forgot about them. That was what he came in to tell us, wasn't it?"

"Not really," said the clairvoyante. "The real reason he came in was to let someone—one of us—know that he had found out (guessed, very probably) that the game we were really playing was murder."

"And how, pray tell, did he arrive at that brilliant deduction?" inquired O. P. sarcastically.

"Through following you to the swimming-pool, Mr. Oliver," she said quietly. "I believe Rapley saw something while he was spying on you—something which probably meant very little to him at the time, but which later, when he'd had time to think about it, seemed odd. As he turned to come back inside, I think he might've seen one of us standing in the lighted window of Miss Cobb's bedroom. Someone who shouldn't have been there. Someone who should've been somewhere else and who, in fact, most of us would've been willing to swear *was* somewhere else."

Bennie made a small choking sound. "I never went near her, I swear it! I don't even know where her bedroom is—I never went up there with you." His eyes widened, his voice shook. "I was in the library, I really was—phoning Mother like I said."

"Yes," said Mrs. Charles. "And it was at this point that Miss Cobb's killer should've abandoned his plans. He improvised beautifully, but the sad truth of the matter is that from then on everything went wrong for him."

"Miss Cobb was *murdered?*" said Cappy in a dismayed voice.

The clairvoyante went on, "And there again nothing went to plan. Miss Cobb obligingly died of heart failure before her killer could carry out his real intention of strangling her with this."

She took the nylon stocking from her pocket and draped it over the arm of her chair. "And in assisting the would-be murderer by dropping dead of shock, Miss Cobb became, if you like, an accessory to murder—the murder of Miss Freda Cobb."

Everyone stared at the stocking. Cappy, the first to raise her eyes, said with a shudder, "Well, thank God nobody can accuse me of killing her. I was in here with all of you."

"But we weren't all in here, were we, petal?" O. P. reminded her. "Not all the time. I certainly wasn't; neither was Faye. Mrs. Charles is the only one who never left the room. . . . Oh, and Leo —he's kosher too. And Danny and Lilla—they're okay; they were only next door in the dining-room—with Cappy, unbeknown to either of them, earwigging at the door." He pursed his lips and solemnly shook his head. "It's Bennie I'm still bothered about. . . . And Bruce and Teddy and Ray. Where were you, Bruce?" he asked him. "Alone in the study did I hear you say? And where were Teddy and Ray when they went missing?"

"I told you before, I was with Bruce," said Teddy quickly.

"Not all the time, you weren't!" Bruce snapped back at him. "I saw you standing in the hall. . . ." Bruce's eyes narrowed. "You looked very suspicious to me. You could've just come back downstairs after frightening the life out of Miss Cobb."

"I'd only just come out of here to look for Bennie," Teddy protested indignantly. "I was standing in the hall trying to find my cigarettes when you suddenly appeared in the study doorway."

"So you say," said Bruce sniffily.

"And we still don't know where Mr. and Mrs. Inch were, do we?" O. P. pointed out to everyone. He looked back at Mrs. Charles, who, after a small pause, continued:

"If we exclude Mr. Rosenberg, who admits to being on his own in the library for a time, Mr. Cummings, who was similarly on his own for a time (in the hall, he claims), Miss Hirsch, who joined Miss Osborne and Danny in the dining-room, and you, Mr. Neville— alone in the study until Mr. Cummings joined you—what we find ourselves left with is the possibility of a conspiracy. Maybe you, Mr. Oliver, as a member of a conspiracy among the people left together for a short time in this room (Mrs. Gould, Mr. Polomka,

Mr. Newman, and myself), slipped upstairs and frightened Miss Cobb to death while Miss Osborne, Miss Hirsch, and Danny were in the dining-room and Mr. Rosenberg was in the library and Mr. Neville was in the study and Mr. and Mrs. Inch were out in the kitchen. Or maybe it was a conspiracy between you and Mrs. Gould. Or was it a conspiracy between Mr. and Mrs. Inch? Did Mr. Inch, say, go upstairs *before* he took up Miss Cobb's warm milk? But then again, if it were a conspiracy, it could just as easily have been Mr. Neville who went up there, with Mr. Cummings as his co-conspirator. Or Rapley. Was he murdered by his co-conspirator who wished to silence him. And what about Miss Osborne and Danny?"

"But I was listening at the door," said Cappy slowly. "I could hear them talking."

"You're quite sure about that?" said Mrs. Charles. "Maybe what you heard was a tape recording of their voices."

Cappy frowned. "Yes, of course, I'm sure it was them—*really* them." She hesitated. Then she said, "Don't you remember? I burst in on them." She turned to Lilla with a scowl. "When you started to run my dancers down."

Lilla made a face, said nothing.

"There wouldn't have been enough time for Danny or Lilla to whiz upstairs and back down again," said O. P. meditatively. "Lilla couldn't have—not on that gammy leg of hers. Always assuming, of course, that she's not been faking it! Cappy was up at that door listening to what they were saying seconds after they went out of here; and she was in there like a shot—probably no more than three or four minutes later."

O. P. paused, looked at Bennie. "Sorry about this, old fruit, but things are beginning to look decidedly black for you, I must say." He turned to Bruce. "And I don't think your story would hold up all that well in court either. I mean, you have been rather more weepy than usual. . . . You're quite sure it's not a guilty conscience that's been upsetting you?"

"Why don't you stop guessing, O. P., and let Mrs. Charles tell us who she thinks it was?" sighed Danny Midas.

O. P. widened his eyes at her. "You know who it was?"

The clairvoyante looked at Danny Midas. "I think it was you, Danny. I think Rapley, when he turned back after following Mr. Oliver to the swimming-pool, looked up at Miss Cobb's bedroom window and saw you when really you should've been downstairs in the dining-room ironing out your problems with Miss Osborne."

"That's ridiculous," Cappy interrupted her. "*I* was in there too, remember."

"I hadn't forgotten. It wasn't until you went in there—soon after —that Danny left you and Miss Osborne squabbling noisily between yourselves to cover up his absence while he slipped upstairs to his sister-in-law's room."

Cappy's pale cheeks grew pink. She spoke furiously. "It's my turn, is it? I'm part of a conspiracy now, am I?"

"Yes, Miss Hirsch. And I'm afraid this was something you let slip quite some time before you joined your co-conspirators, Danny and Miss Osborne, in the dining-room—as had been prearranged among the three of you. Miss Osborne played her part perfectly. I would never have suspected her—perhaps not even all three of you—if it hadn't been for you, Miss Hirsch. . . . Something you and you alone did when you first arrived here last night. You walked into this room and immediately removed your cloak. An innocent, automatic act, perhaps . . . But I don't really think so, Miss Hirsch. Not now . . . You knew—or rather you were the only one to betray that you knew—that you were here to stay. And you shouldn't have known that, not if everything Danny had told me about his fears for his life were true. The driver of your bus knew what was going on, so did Mr. Neville and the Inches, Miss Cobb, Rapley, and myself. And Danny, of course. But no one else, he assured me."

Lilla looked at Cappy and smiled faintly. "I warned you about her," she said.

"Oh, shut up," said Cappy irritably. "I overheard, didn't I? I was listening at the door of the administrative office at the theatre, and I heard Danny and Bruce discussing what they were going to do to us."

Bruce said, "Well, that's interesting. We deliberately never discussed it at the theatre."

Leo looked very worried, as if he could see his whole bright new future slipping slowly away from him. "I'm sure there's been some terrible mistake," he said. "Why would Danny want to kill his sister-in-law?"

Mrs. Charles addressed her reply to Danny Midas. "For the reason you gave everyone for bringing them here the way you did.

. . . Not that it was true that you believed your life was in danger —you deluded us all there—but because of your wife, Jo, your fears about her. It was a very anxious time for Miss Cobb while she and I waited for all of you to arrive last night, not because she was nervous about the trick you, Danny, were playing on everyone, but because she was terrified that in the meanwhile she might confess something to me. You do not need me to tell you that your sister-in-law was going mad, Danny. Nor do you need me to tell you that it was fear and guilt that were slowly driving her out of her mind."

Mrs. Charles paused, her eyes never left his face. Then, a little sadly: "She knew your wife was dead. And this was why, when you pretended that someone was trying to kill you, she insisted on your calling in someone like me, a clairvoyante, and not the police. She was terrified, wasn't she? that they would find the body, the body she knew was hidden somewhere here in this house or its grounds. Her poor mind was so tormented and confused by fear and guilt that she couldn't cope with the thought of the changes a discovery like that would make to her life. She would've gone to any lengths —and in fact had in the past when she effectively put an end to your affair with Faye Gould by giving her cause to believe that she was your wife—to keep everything just as it was."

Bennie, his face shiny with perspiration, asked, "Are you saying she murdered Danny's wife?"

"No." Mrs. Charles shook her head. "I think Danny killed her— strangled her with a nylon stocking when she told him she was leaving him." She looked at Danny Midas. "I very much doubt that Miss Cobb knew for sure that you'd killed Jo. This, I think, was what was driving her mad. . . . The fear she had that you had killed Jo and the inner conflict brought about by this terrible expectation that this was what you'd done to her sister and not knowing for sure if she were right. Nobody gets the better of you, she told me. . . . An observation she'd made over the years that she'd lived under your roof, and it was this, I feel, which slowly convinced her that her sister wouldn't have bettered you either."

Mrs. Charles regarded him quizzically. "Was there ever a meeting between Miss Cobb and your wife in a railway station buffet after Jo had allegedly left you, or was this too just another part of the illusion you were creating?"

There was a deathly silence, broken only by the distant sound of vehicles moving slowly on the drive.

At length Bruce said quietly, "That's them now—the police. They're here. The coach is back too."

Hawkes knocked softly and then poked his head round the door and looked at Danny Midas. "Would you mind coming along with me now, sir? Inspector Jordan's just arrived and would like a word with you before taking a look at the deceased."

Danny nodded and went out.

The room was very quiet. Then O. P. began to chuckle. Bennie gave him a hostile look. "I can't see that there's anything to laugh about."

"Oh, come on now," O. P. laughed. "Don't you know when you've had your leg pulled. It's like Mrs. Charles said—it's all part of an illusion. And if I may say so, one of Danny's better ones. None of it's real. It's only a game, Bennie!"

"I doubt that my boy is going to get up and stop playing dead now that the game is over," said Mrs. Inch bitterly.

"Or Miss Cobb and Faye," Ray Newman gravely reminded O. P. "Danny does some strange things—and I don't doubt that this all started out as a game—but even he would've called things off after what happened to them."

"Rubbish," said O. P. "What happened there merely gave an added fillip to proceedings. He improvised round them."

"You're sick, O. P.," said Cappy disgustedly. "Sick in the head."

They glared at one another. Then, abruptly, the tension was broken by a single, sharp, whip-cracking sound.

Bruce started forward. "That was a shot," he said.

He rushed to the door and threw it open. The others quickly followed him. Ahead of them, running towards the open study door, was Hawkes. There was no sign of any other police officer, the Inspector Jordan he had mentioned a few minutes earlier.

Bruce paused in the study doorway. The others crowded behind him. Hawkes was bent over Danny Midas, who was sitting doubled across his desk. A revolver nestled in the hand resting on the blood-spattered sheet of blotting paper under his head.

"Oh my God," whispered Bruce. "He's blown his brains out."

Hawkes looked up, as if suddenly aware that he was not alone. He looked greatly distressed. His hands were trembling. "He asked me to wait a moment. He said there was something he had to do. He said he wouldn't keep me more than a minute."

With the exception of Bruce and Bennie, who remained standing in the doorway, the others filed silently into the room.

O. P. looked at Mrs. Charles and frowned. "I guess he really did kill his wife and Miss Cobb after all, didn't he?"

She made no reply.

Cappy said nervously, "Well, I'll admit that he left the room while Lilla and I were arguing. But we didn't know why he went out, did we, Lilla? I thought it was because he was fed up with listening to us. I didn't know he was going to kill his sister-in-law."

"Yes," said the clairvoyante, "and I might've believed you too if it hadn't been for what happened to Faye Gould. Faye didn't commit suicide, Miss Hirsch. You killed her. It was you who stole Mr. Neville's gun, wasn't it? You had it all the time. . . . Concealed in your purse, no doubt. And when you went out to the cloakroom to see what was keeping Miss Osborne and you found Faye there, you simply made the most of your opportunity and shot her. Then, remembering what she'd told you earlier of her neurotic fear, you quickly made it look as if she'd panicked because she'd been unable to get the door open and shot herself. It wasn't a premeditated murder, although I believe you knew intuitively that something might go wrong with the plans Danny had made for last night. So you took out a little personal insurance and stole Mr. Neville's gun."

Cappy laughed at her. "Why would I want to kill Faye?"

"I think you were seriously alarmed by her hysterical outburst upstairs in Miss Cobb's bedroom. It was a side of her you'd never seen before, and you suddenly saw her as a potential threat to your future plans—the ones you had made with Danny Midas and Miss Osborne. Particularly if Faye were still in love with Danny."

"Me make plans with *her?*" Cappy flung a contemptuous look at Lilla. "You're madder than I thought! There's no way that old hag's going to figure in *my* future, I can tell you that! The only plan I've got in regard to her is never to see her again for as long as I live."

"I don't think that's very likely. . . ." said Mrs. Charles with a faint smile. "That you and Miss Osborne will never see one another again. Miss Osborne is your aunt."

Cappy looked hard at her. "You've got an even better imagination than Danny Midas had!"

"The photograph on the wall—the one of Danny with Miss Osborne's brother and another young seaman." Mrs. Charles went up to the photograph and stood before it. "I knew I'd seen you somewhere before—your likeness—and I had. Here in this photograph. Miss Osborne's brother is your father, isn't he?"

"Save your breath, Cappy," said Lilla tiredly. "It's all over. You might just as well face it. It was a nice try, but you lost."

Hawkes cleared his throat and then said in an unsteady voice, "I think, if you wouldn't mind, please, ladies and gentlemen, that you should all return to the drawing-room while I go and let Inspector Jordan in."

He went to the study door and waited until they had all moved out into the hall. Leo hung back, touched Mrs. Charles lightly on the arm as she passed him. She turned to him questioningly. He looked hurt and indignant. "You lied to me about the second bullet hole, the one in the toilet door. You said Cappy's explanation was perfectly logical." He spoke softly but accusingly.

"And so it was, Mr. Polomka. But as is often the way with these things, there could also have been another equally logical explanation for the bullet hole in the door. For Faye to have committed suicide, there would have to be traces of powder burns on her hand." Slowly, she shook her head. "But for that second shot, Mr. Polomka, I doubt that the police would've found any such traces. Faye didn't fire the shot which killed her. And hence the need, wouldn't you agree? for her killer to place the murder weapon in her hand after she'd been shot and fire the gun a second time—somewhere safe, like into the solid wood of a heavy oak door."

"I refuse to believe that Cappy could do such a terrible thing," said Leo stoutly. "I think your mind must be horribly twisted to think these terrible things about people."

Mrs. Charles was taken aback by the look on his face. He hated her. There could be no mistake about it. He did not care what Danny Midas had done; he cared even less about Cappy, the crime she had committed. All that mattered to Leo Polomka was Leo Polomka, the shattering of his hopes and dreams.

He wheeled about and walked quickly away from her.

Epilogue

Mrs. Charles walked slowly towards the drawing-room. Inch was waiting for her at the door. The others had gone in.

As she drew near him, he reached inside his jacket and withdrew a long, narrow envelope. "This is for you, madam," he said gravely. "Mr. Midas instructed me that I was either to give it to you, in the event of his death, or to return it to him should he ask me for it."

Inch paused momentarily. Then he went on, "I think Mr. Midas wrote the letter while you were interviewing everyone. He pretended he had some business to attend to, some papers to go through in the study, and that he might just as well get on with that as sit about wasting time in the kitchen drinking tea." His voice tailed off. Then, gently: "I think he knew, madam—just as Miss Osborne knew—that you were going to find out the truth."

She took the envelope, opened it. Inch watched her for a moment, then quietly opened the drawing-room door and discreetly disappeared.

She began to read.

Dear 'Del,

If you are reading this, then that can only mean that I am dead as it was on this condition that Inch was to give my letter to you.

I will not pretend to you. I do not want to die, and it is something that I will strenuously avoid—to the bitter end, one might say. I shall watch you closely, and when I am sure—*if* I am sure—there is to be no other way out, then I shall not hesitate to do what I know must be done.

There are so many things I had forgotten about you, 'Del. Principally, your capacity to observe and listen—so unusual these days. But then we were married for so short a time,

weren't we? An hour? Or was it an hour and a half before that
absolute tigress of a mother of yours snatched you back and
spirited you off to Italy and your family there while she set
about procuring an annulment?

It might have worked for us, but then again, when I look at
you now and then see myself—what I have become—I doubt
it. I think your mother knew what she was doing. (I seem to
remember that she too was clairvoyant!) Sometimes I even
wonder if it ever really happened. It was all so long ago.

Did I lie to you in those days? I cannot remember, but I
hope not. And I would like you to believe me when I say that I
had no wish to lie to you now. It was forced upon me. I had no
alternative once Freda saw your name in that newspaper
article we discussed over the telephone last week, and I rashly
told her that I knew you slightly. (Again the truth, we only
ever knew one another slightly—your mother saw to that!)

Freda, as you are no doubt aware, was quite mad. Obsessed
with an idea. The belief that I had killed Jo. (True, as it happens, though Freda and I never discussed it with one another.)

It all happened exactly as I described it to you when you
interviewed me. Jo walked out on me without leaving a note
or telling me she was going and returned to her home town.
From the railway station she telephoned her sister, Freda (or
rather a family friend on whom she could rely to be discreet—
Jo's parents were still alive at the time and her father certainly
would have killed her for defying him if he could have laid
hands on her). Freda met Jo at the station buffet and gave her
some money, and Freda—ever the one for a nagging conscience—insisted that Jo should do the decent thing and return to me and tell me to my face that it was all over between
us.

I do not know why Jo did as Freda asked. Maybe she had
second thoughts and wanted time to think and be sure that
this was what she really wanted, or maybe she was concerned
that she might not be able to call on Freda again for help in
the future if she did not "do the right thing" by me. Anyway,
she came back, and I killed her. Quite deliberately, no fuss, no
frills, and with no regrets. I would do it all over again, exactly
the same thing. My only defence can be that I had lost you,
and I had lost Lilla (I daresay you know all about that too!), and

I had no intention of losing her. I felt cheated, 'Del, if you can understand that. I wanted so little from her. Just a home, her to be in it, and a son. Was that really too much to ask? I did not think so at the time, and I still don't. But that is not important now. I must concern myself with the future—something I should have done years ago but couldn't because of Freda.

You were right about the note. It was an old one of Jo's that I had kept—one she had written to me soon after we married. It referred, of course, to my career, and not to the show *Abracadabra*. She used to joke about it, that I would never make it to the top. (Perhaps this was even why she really left me, because of her lack of faith in my ability to become a big name in the entertainment world.) I arranged for the note to be delivered to the theatre the night I was there with Freda. All magicians are actors—the good ones are, anyway—so it was no problem for me to put on a convincing act to hoodwink Freda into believing that I was shocked and frightened by the note. Though I knew I was on fairly safe ground. Jo—anything touching on her—was always Freda's Achilles' heel. The mere mention of her name was enough to send her into a blind panic.

The stranger who supposedly called here last Thursday night while Freda and I were alone together in the house and frightened me by firing off blank shots did not exist. It was all on tape—the whole thing from beginning to end, timed to start a few minutes after Freda had settled down to watch one of her favourite television programmes. I knew she would not stir herself to answer the door when the bell "rang." It is a hobby of mine, tape-recording people's conversations with me. (Was this one of the things you discovered about me, or did I succeed in deceiving you here?) In this instance, I merely took most of the sounds I needed off one of those cop programmes on TV and then added a touch or two of my own—like recording Bruno's bark and then adding that to the tape so that it sounded as if he was chasing the get-away car down the drive. By the time Freda got to the door, it was all over. Her fears about Jo—that anything that happened concerning Jo would result in people finding out that she was dead, murdered by me—blinded Freda, deluded her into seeing what was never there.

It is quite true what Bruce said about me. I enjoy playing psychological tricks on people. I like wearing people down, watching their reactions, enjoying it all. Not very nice when one sees it all written down as baldly as this. But it is true, I do get a perverse pleasure out of watching people jockeying for position, seeing them become anxious and scared. (Was it this unlovable trait, I wonder, that your mother spotted in me and objected to so strongly? Or maybe it was my ruthless streak. For which I make no apology. Without it I would never have gone as far as I have as a highly successful professional entertainer.)

Cappy has got the same streak in her. I doubt that we will be happy. (You will note that I am still optimistic that this letter will never be read by you, and that the plans we three made—Cappy, Lilla, and I—in Las Vegas will come to fruition.) But I am tired and—yes, just fed up enough that I am willing to take that risk. I shall go forward (hopefully!) into our marriage with no mistaken conceptions about her. She is ambitious—as I was at her age—and impatient. That too was one of my faults. I am Cappy's short cut to where she wants to go professionally, and so long as she keeps her side of our bargain and gives me the son I want, I will have no complaints. I have no mistaken conceptions about marriage any more either, 'Del. The "pipe and slippers round the cosy log fire" was only ever a dream. Unreal and never meant for me. All I want is a son. That now is my one driving ambition, the only thing that really matters to me.

As for Lilla, you must not be too hard on her. You have probably guessed that she is—or has been—a desperately sick woman. Chemotherapy has given her a remission—hopefully a full cure—but huge private medical bills have crippled her financially. She was heavily in debt and would have been for years to come but for me. All she had to do to repay me was to help Cappy and me get what we wanted by giving me an alibi, vouching that I was in the dining-room with her and Cappy when Freda died.

Freda, as you will no doubt appreciate, was in no frame of mind to let me marry anybody. She had stepped in between Faye and me, and I knew that the moment she got wind of what I had in mind for Cappy and me, she would find some way of stopping us. Though it would not have been possible for her to come between us in the way that she had when it was Faye I had wanted to marry. After all there were no secrets between Cappy and me. There couldn't be. But nevertheless, Freda's mental state was making her more dangerous by the minute, especially since she found out that I had secretly divorced Jo. (I had to do this, get a divorce from my wife before I could remarry; only I knew for certain that Jo was dead, and this was how I intended things to remain. As a legally divorced man no one could show just cause why I should not marry again.)

Freda would never have let go, 'Del. She was like the Old Man of the Sea in the story of Sinbad the Sailor. She had entwined herself round my neck, and the only way out for me was to do as Sinbad had done. I had to kill her to be rid of her. *Abracadabra*—the musical based on my life—gave me the opportunity I sought. By ensuring that Jo was portrayed in the worst possible light, I knew no one would question her alleged desire for revenge. (Some would even say I asked for it!) Freda's real fear (over and above her knowing, or rather *suspecting*, that I had murdered Jo) would, I think, have been that someone other than herself knew or had guessed the truth about Jo. This for Freda was probably a far more frightening prospect to contemplate than if it had been Jo herself who was threatening her comfortable, if not exactly easy existence.

There was another factor to consider too. The challenge it presented to me. And I will be honest about it, the whole idea excited me as nothing else has done in quite a long time. Here was my opportunity to create an illusion worthy of the old greats in magic. . . . The old-time illusionists who, with a full company of assistants, filled the stage with spectacle and colour and, the most important ingredient of all, confusion.

I visualized how it was back in those days. . . . A stage full of people all engaged in different activities, the illusionist (the great man himself!) the focal point . . . First one thing happens, then another—this appears, that disappears!—the stage is full of colourful activity, chaos and confusion reigns with assistants rushing about here, there, and everywhere, clamouring for everybody's attention—the members of the audience convinced they have never taken their eyes off the illusionist—the illusionist (out of sight but usually by means of sound) fostering this conviction. Only he's not there any more and hasn't been for some time. Everything that has taken place on stage has been merely a tactic to divert attention from him. Then, all of a sudden, he makes his dramatic reappearance—in the case of the old-time illusionists, maybe at the back of the theatre, or he will disrobe and reveal himself to be one of his stage assistants. *And yet everyone watching will swear that he was the one person who never left centre stage.*

This then was to be my illusion, that everyone would swear that I had never stepped out of the spotlight.

I only wish I had known it was going to be so easy to kill Freda; I would have done it long ago. Her doctor had warned me that she could go at any minute. He also said she could live for years. Outlive me, in fact. This latter absolutely terrifying prospect, from my point of view, made up my mind. I chose the same method I had used to kill Jo—strangulation—and I can't tell you how surprised I was when Freda simply dropped dead of fright. Again that weird twist, quirk, in my character . . . There would have been no satisfaction in simply killing Freda. I wanted the pleasure of watching her reaction, of seeing her face when I opened Pandora's Box, as it were, and she saw Jo's body, the absolute irrefutable confirmation of all her worst fears.

I have always believed that Freda thought I poisoned Jo and disposed of her body, either in lime or buried somewhere in the grounds—a notion, I confess, that I, as an avid gardener, actively encouraged. (That unpleasant bent in my character again, I regret to say.) She used to walk in the grounds sometimes with her dog, looking at this shrub and that, with a most peculiar expression on her face. Other times she would spend ages in the potting-shed—doing heaven knows what, but possibly going through the range of weed killers (poisons) I keep out there trying to determine which one I might have used to kill Jo. (I must say I have always enjoyed the idea of this latter possibility immensely.)

Jo's body was, of course, in none of the places Freda thought of looking. It is in the chest, the old wooden trunk with all the paraphernalia that went with Danny Midas' early act. Which will no doubt explain why it has always been my express wish that the trunk should be buried at sea with my ashes. Freda never once suspected, not even when I had Bruce and Rapley bring the trunk down from the attic and position it across the connecting door between Freda's room and the one you were to occupy. That was one dirty trick even Freda would never have accused me of playing on anyone. Her limited imagination (in all but the one respect!) would not have been able to encompass the idea that anyone could be quite so daring. But daring to do things right under people's noses is what being a good magician is all about, isn't it? I do it all the time, and even if I say so myself, I am good at it. The best!

It was all planned between us—Lilla, Cappy, and me—that Lilla would take me on one side, into the library (though it became necessary to improvise here when Bennie used the phone in there to make his call). Everyone would know why Lilla wanted to talk to me privately. She and Cappy had been deliberately at one another's throats for weeks. It would be quite reasonable to expect that sooner or later one of them would demand a showdown with me. Nor would anyone be terribly surprised when Cappy eavesdropped at the door and then burst in on us.

Lilla and Cappy's extreme state of nervous tension heightened their performances which—up to the point where I felt it was safe for me to slip away and carry out my "errand"— were really quite brilliant, I thought. The squabbling between them was such a routine, boring occurrence that none of the creative team would have thought twice about it.

Fortunately for me, I did not run into Bennie—he had closed the library door behind him when he went in there. Inch, I knew, would not go near Freda for the best part of an hour after she had retired (and the arrangement between Freda and myself was that she would excuse herself and go up to bed as soon as I arrived). Rapley—if he had carried out my instructions—should have been in the servants' quarters, and Bruce was where I had told him to remain until I sent for him. (Though even he, like Rapley, did not follow instructions and bumped into Teddy Cummings in the hall!) I saw nobody but Freda. I hurried upstairs to the guest-room (your room), quickly dragged the trunk clear, then unlocked it and raised the lid. Then I unlocked the connecting door and knocked on it. Freda came up to it—she thought it was you—and called out to me (you) to come in. I did not respond, and after a few moments she opened the door and stepped forward expecting to see you.

Her face, 'Del, was a picture. I can find no words to describe it, nor could any words of mine do justice to the satisfaction I received from watching her gaze drop to the trunk. Suffice it to say that nothing, not even Freda's death, has ever given me such exquisite pleasure. I doubt that Freda saw me. Then suddenly she stumbled backwards into her room with her hands clutched to her breast, and it was all over. She dropped dead. As neatly and cleanly as that. I know that I took a terrible risk here in that she might have cried out. I gambled that she wouldn't, that the shock of what she had seen would strike her dumb. I had to have this moment of pleasure, regardless of the risk I was taking over it. This was my reward for all the years she had forced me to waste, all the years I have had to sit and watch her watching me. . . . The man for whom she had a question which she wanted but did not dare to ask.

Afterwards I simply closed and relocked the door, then quickly shut up the trunk and locked it again and then pushed it back to the door. Then I went swiftly round to her room, drew the curtains, and picked her up off the floor—she had collapsed too close to the connecting door for comfort, it looked suspicious—and laid her out on her bed to look as though she had collapsed there.

I confess that here I might have made two mistakes. The first that Freda shed one of her shoes, either when she stumbled back from the connecting door, or when I picked her up. In my excitement—and I was very excited, even more tense than when I go out in front of the TV cameras or on stage—I did not notice the missing shoe. But you did. I asked Inch why you had remained behind in Freda's room, and he told me about the shoe you had picked up. I am also wondering if it was you who found the nylon stocking I had intended to use to strangle Freda with. The bedside table—I think this might have been where I dropped it while I saw to the curtains. In my haste to be done, I forgot to pick it up. . . . My second mistake, and only time will tell how serious it will prove for me. Inch made no reference to it, and I certainly could not query either him or Mrs. Inch about it (if it were she who had found it and perhaps slipped it away somewhere in one of the drawers in Freda's room).

After I had arranged Freda on the bed, I went quickly downstairs, cut the telephone wires to create a further atmosphere of mutual mistrust and confusion among my assembled company of players, and then rejoined Lilla and Cappy, convinced that I was home and dry and that nobody had seen me leave the dining-room, that everybody would swear I had been in there all the time.

My confidence here was justified. No one indoors saw me leave or return to the dining-room. Neither would any of the people who, without my knowledge, were wandering about out of doors—Faye, O. P., and Rapley—have known anything about my visit to Freda's room if I had not gone near the window. My other mistakes were through sheer carelessness, but the one I made here was downright stupid, done automatically, without thinking. Rapley saw me drawing the curtains, though I had no inkling of this until he came into the drawing-room and announced that the rotor arms of the two cars were missing. This, 'Del, was not part of my illusion. I was as baffled as the next person by their disappearance—that is, until Rapley made reference to the ticking off I had given him at the theatre for dereliction of duty, which he suggested Cappy might have overheard. I guessed then that he had seen something (though I had no idea what), and that he had removed the rotor arms himself, thereby making it impossible for him to fetch the police until he and I had had a little chat about his long-term future in the employ of Danny Midas. The brazen manner in which he picked up my cue as to when and where we should meet to have our talk was, I felt, a good indication of the kind of problem he was going to prove to be in time to come. The willingness he expressed to fetch in the dog was his way of telling me that he had got my message and that he was happy to accept my invitation to meet at the wood later. And I must say I admired his cool. It was pure Danny Midas. I say it

Illusion

myself. I could not have handled it better or with more aplomb.

We met, as arranged, near the wood after everyone else had gone upstairs. Rapley did not appear at all concerned that I was carrying a shotgun—he had seen me often enough with one and probably never even noticed it. I let him tell me what he had seen and what he now suspected—most of it guess-work but nevertheless uncomfortably accurate. And then I shot him. As with Jo, no fuss, no frills! I did not hear Inch approaching us until he was almost right on top of me. I barely had time to dive safely out of sight under cover of some bushes. He looked at Rapley, lifted him up, and saw that he had been shot in the chest, and then he went back to the house.

As swiftly as I could, I then left the shotgun under Rapley's body—there was no time to do this before—and then, as luck would have it, there was that gnarled root sticking up out of the ground nearby—just the sort of thing someone might trip and fall over in the dark—and I scuffed it up with the toe of my shoe to make it look as though this was exactly what had happened to Rapley with the shotgun going off accidentally as a result. Then I hurried back to the house, keeping well clear of the front of it—I could see Inch standing dazedly on the terrace, not knowing what to do next—slipped quickly and quietly inside to the study (you were standing at the front door looking out at something—Inch perhaps), changed out of my mackintosh and shoes (I had left a fresh change of outer clothing there specially for this purpose), and took another shotgun from the gun cupboard. Then, stepping out into the hall with it, I pretended to be every bit as confused and alarmed as the rest of you were by the sudden explosion which had disturbed everyone.

So there you have it all. The why and the how.

About Faye I can say little other than that it never should have happened. Cappy over-reacted there, and if our plans fall down anywhere, it will be here, with the bullet hole in the toilet door. The one you didn't like! You saw it, 'Del, and so will the police, and if it bothered you—and I know it did—it will bother them, and they have the means at their disposal to satisfy their doubts.

Yes, on reflection I would say that this is where it really all went wrong. Not with Rapley—I would defy anybody to prove that he died other than accidentally—nor with Freda who died of a bad heart, but with Faye and the second time Cappy had to fire Bruce's gun with it pressed into Faye's hand so that the police would find traces of powder burns on her flesh.

I had no idea that Cappy had stolen Bruce's gun. If I had known, I would have taken it away from her before she could do any harm with it.

I guess this was the biggest mistake of all—that I did not keep my threat to Bruce and make him hand over the gun months ago. He only carried it about with him because he liked to fantasize about killing me with it one day.

I never thought he would, but believe it or not, 'Del, I am actually beginning to think he has!

Yours with no regrets, except about you,

Danny Midas.

About the Author

Mignon Warner was born in Australia, but now lives in England with her husband, whom she assists in the invention, design, and manufacture of magic apparatus. She spends most of her free time pursuing her interest in psychic research and the occult. Her previous novels about the clairvoyante Mrs. Charles include *Devil's Knell, The Girl Who Was Clairvoyant,* and *Death in Time.*